I0598600

Apertambuxtion

By: Anthony Reif

In Association With
Living Beyond Life, LLC

DEDICATION

This book is dedicated to everyone who is in it
and to everyone who supported its creation.
It is also dedicated to Living Beyond Life,
a quest to reach and achieve the unknown.
It will all make sense one day.

CONTENTS

Acknowledgments

Author's Note

ACKNOWLEDGMENTS

This book was written with the help of
my connection to the other side.
John wouldn't have it any other way.

AUTHOR'S NOTE

I would have liked the cover to feature Mary Jane with green hair facing the readers. There would be a view of the beach and Chateau in the background with Howard somewhere in the distance and a faded picture of the Masked Man sitting on his throne while young John is meditating.

I would even settle for a picture of Mary Jane in the dark (she will be visible and still facing readers). This is from the scene in the beginning where she hands John the chocolate. For now, it is just a mysterious matte black book with green lettering reading, "Apertambuxtion."

As the author, I am happy that someone is reading this book and hope you enjoy it as much as I did writing it. Please spread the word and join the quest to live beyond life.

Here follows the first adventure of John, Mary Jane, Howard, and the Chocolate. That is what this is. The rest will come in time.

Chapter 1

The Catalyst

Apertambuxtion. Ah-pur-tam-bux-tee-uhn. That is the password for his computer. He was worried people would mispronounce it given the opportunity. It was a word that would stick in his mind like a thumbtack. Who exactly is he anyway? That is not important. He prefers not to use names to avoid association and attachment. His name is John. It is always short lived when John wants to keep his name from people. Social niceties somehow override his own intentions, because he doesn't want to appear unforthcoming.

Going through his email John came upon the word of the day. Ferhoodle. It went as quickly as it came, at this introduction of a new word. Ferhoodle. What had the first one been? Peri-something. Periwinkle? No. It was a new word. Now fallen into oblivion, the password for John's computer was lost. (The reader will note that it is still written in this book, but John didn't know that.) If you have been on a computer with an Internet connection that can't keep up with the six tabs open on your browser, you will understand his frustration. We will come to see that the reason John needs his password is a more pressing matter in the future, but for right now, he is already late for work.

With less urgent matters at hand, John shutdown his computer and raced to the door so he wouldn't get yelled at by his boss, who still thought that being five minutes late was the end of the world. John wanted to see what would happen if it really was the end of the world. He could imagine his boss still being on time, opening the doors of the store to reveal a post-apocalyptic wasteland where the customers never came even though he was on time. People like to hold on to what they think is important, even after they have lost everything. That didn't make any sense to John. John couldn't even hold on to it while it was there.

"JOHN!" his boss said towering over him as he walked into the store. "You are late again! You know what they say about people who are late." John didn't know what they say about people who are late, but he didn't think it was relevant to any real-life situation anyway, so he didn't care to find out. He nodded to his boss, and quickly walking by the tall, overweight man, commented that he was sorry and would never do it again. Like it was his choice. His boss saw it as a decision to do things like that, be early, be late, not end up in the hospital on work days. Everybody knows someone who takes his job too seriously.

John was on the verge of a breakthrough. Though he didn't know it yet, his whole life was about to change. A needed change. A wanted change. Nothing in life was the way he was told it would be. John was ready for this next step, but not the abrupt nature of the change. People are so scared of change. They believe in permanence. They are pretty confident in thinking that what they just saw will still be there when they turn around, or while their back is turned to it. People trust that everything is just the way they left it, even when they have no proof, beside a distant memory that may not have existed in the first place. Most people remember the wrong colors in their memories. It has been shown that fabricated memories can be just as real as the ones we believe we experienced. Memories can only exist in the present moment. The mind creates reality, just as John and his boss were doing that very moment.

The catalyst. There is always a catalyst. Something that breaks everything apart; starts the interruption of reality. Once in a while, people are lucky enough for their own mind to be the catalyst into the real world, but most of them end up in an institution. One could argue that Mary Jane was not the catalyst into John's new perception, but it would be just as easy to let facts be and stop worrying more about identification than the story that is to come.

As this girl with green hair walked into the store, John felt his breath tighten, like someone had taken the air out of the room. Everything seemed frozen in that eternal instant where John was standing still and holding his breath. It hadn't been intentional, certain life changing events seem to have this effect on a person. There was a faint remembrance of smoke fading out of his mouth as he finished that first breath. Alarm bells. Ringing. Panic. Everything was gone, but he was still there surrounded by it. The energy was still floating around him like a scent. John was jolted back into reality, after hardly a moment had passed in the material world he was supposed to be tending to.

"Can I help you find anything today?" he asked the green haired girl.

"John -ohn -hn -hn -hn," his name echoed and reverberated as she spoke it. The color started draining from the room, which was fading into a dark gray. "You know why I am here," she said. "It is time for change." The feeling that went through John is practically indescribable to someone who has not gone so far. The blood in his body, all of his density in fact, seemed to flow into his feet as his body floated upward, like someone wearing cement shoes at the bottom of the ocean. John didn't know if he was breathing, but even if he was, what was it that was entering his body. Energy. John could feel every molecule of his body. Down to the tiniest detail of the brown spot on his hand to the blood vessels running through the veins in his neck. He could see every part of himself, as if he was the universe.

"JOHN!" his boss broke the magic with another scolding. John came crashing to the floor, and jumped up, quickly trying to make it seem normal. "You idiot, you've been standing there with that glazed look on your face for twenty minutes, now you can't even stand up properly."

"I," John started, but he was interrupted by the "puah" that came out of his boss's mouth when something hit him from behind, throwing the man across the room. There was a strange looking man standing where his boss had been seconds before. The man looked like some kind of futuristic nerd from a science fiction TV show, but without the dark sunglasses. He had short hair that was spiked, and dark shiny clothing. Most people, given time to think about it, would have thought the words, "sci-fi greaser." The most noticeable thing to John was his complexion. He seemed to be glowing through his pale skin. Not that glow you get when you are infatuated, but an apparition of visible light that felt like it shouldn't be on this plane, was emanating from the man. A film reel popped up in John's head. It was the YouTube video he had watched a few weeks before of people in movies saying that famous line - Get out of there!

When you have seen as many movies as John, life seems like one big setup. It was never hard to predict what would happen next, but here was John in the real world wondering how he was going to get out of this one.

The Futuristic Man walked toward John with his hand glowing so profusely it seemed a ball of light was gathering in his palm. It turns out it was. John jumped out of the way as the ball of light flew towards him and blew up a nearby display rack. This doesn't happen in real life, John barely had time to think to himself, before running from the next explosion. Then came the humming. Hmmmmmmmmmmm. It filled the air. It filled his mind. Mmmmmmmmmm. It was a powerful vibration that silenced his mind, and felt comforting to him.

"Apertambuxtion," said a sharp nosed professor as he tapped his stick on the chalkboard, where the word had been written out in chalk. "Are you even paying attention?" said the professor to John, not looking for a response so much as pointing out his lack of attentiveness to the rest of the class. John was sitting at a desk in the classroom with a vague feeling that he was somewhere else. "This may very well be the most important lesson you ever learn, and here you are daydreaming," continued the professor.

"Sometimes I wonder why I even bother trying to teach you anything. This could save your life you know, Apertambux..." the classroom disappeared. John was now sitting on the toilet... with that feeling that he wasn't really there going to the bathroom. He had the feeling before, but now was completely convinced this really wasn't the space he was occupying. The word still floating in his head, Apertambuxtion. What was this all about? Hadn't he heard the word before? The humming started again before his world changed once again. John was now on a beach wearing a white robe, not understanding any of this, still with remnants of the feeling that he was about to die, but also wondering where his other outfit had gone. He imagined the clothes... were they more or less valuable than these robes. What about the contents of the pockets?

A man with a dark, well-trimmed goatee appeared in front of John, with both of his hands in prayer posture at his chest. "Ahh," said the man, "you've come at last. I am here to teach you. But you must listen closely as we don't have much time."

"Apertam..." John started, but the man cut him off in the middle of the word.

"Stop! Don't say it. You don't know how to use it yet and you need my help to get out of the store." How did he know about the store? Was that really the most confusing part? John wondered if this is what happens when you die. "Hold up your two fingers together like this," said the man, demonstrating with his own. John obeyed and lifted his two fingers. "Good. Now hit this frequency. Hmmmmmmm." John didn't see how this was going to help him at all, but what choice did he have? It seemed better than any idea John had thought of, mostly because John had thought of nothing. He started to make the Hmmm sound, and when he started, it filled him completely. His mind, his world, his very being, everything became the sound. Hmmmmmmmm.

John was standing in the store again, but now his hand was up and he was humming as the man had told him. Though John knew where he was from the noise and sounds, he didn't dare open his eyes. If he did he would have seen another ball of light from the Futuristic Man's hand heading right toward him. The energy struck John, but he didn't explode like the rest of the store. He felt himself being pulled away backwards, his eyes still closed. Then he remembered to breathe. Air filled his lungs, but it wasn't the smoldering air of the store, it was something new. Sweet. Refreshing.

Chapter 2
The Girl & The Book

"It's okay John. You did it. The energy was used to bring you here, instead of spewing your atoms into the atmosphere." It was a pleasant voice, a girl's voice. John opened his eyes and saw the green haired girl standing in front of him smiling. He then realized his awkward pose and quickly put down his hand.

"I don't know how you knew to do that," she said, "but you did it just in time." She had a beautiful smile.

"I don't know what is going on," John said, feeling completely lost as to what had happened (and seemed to still be happening).

"It's okay, everything will come in time. Most of it you have to remember on your own, but I will teach you what I can," she replied. "My name is Mary Jane."

"My name is John," said John, breaking his own decision of remaining nameless, with no regard for his own beliefs.

"We already know that John," said Mary Jane, with a slight laugh. Not only had John betrayed his own belief of remaining namelessness, he did it unnecessarily. This should have been the least of John's worries after the events that so recently occurred, and that was the problem. There was no more world. John's whole idea of this existence had been shattered. Just like that. One minute he was late for work, being yelled at by an overbearing authority figure, and the next thing he knew, someone was trying to kill him, as he skipped through various places in space, maybe even time for all he knew. Was that possible? It seemed to have happened anyway, even if it wasn't. To say the least, it was confusing.

"It's okay John," Mary Jane said, as if reading his mind. "I am here to explain it to you. Well, as much as I am allowed to at least."

John was still considering whether or not to trust this green haired beauty, and decided it was the best option he had because for all he knew the Futuristic Man would be waiting outside to kill him. There was something about the way she looked at him. As if she knew him... intimately. John could see she was holding something back. Have you ever had that feeling when you know somebody likes you, but you have no idea who they are? That is how John felt, and it wasn't the first time. Throughout his life he had been having weird experiences that his mind passed off as normal. People he didn't know would tell him how great he was going to become, and others would stare at him intently as he walked by them, once in a while winking in his direction. When is the last time you saw someone wink at you? It seemed the whole world was in on the secret that John himself had yet to discover.

"There is only tonight for me to tell you as much as I can," said Mary Jane. "You'll have to trust me. I don't know if there is anything I can say right now to make this easier, but somewhere in your heart, in your soul, you can feel that we have a connection. You know me. I can't tell you how I know it, but there is a feeling I have that I can see is budding inside of you as well. It is instinctual. It's because time does not progress as you think it does. Everything between us has already happened, even though the possibility didn't even exist a few hours ago. For now I need you to trust me, because I know a lot more than you do about this, and I want you to know how meaningful it is to both of us."

'Is she coming on to me,' John thought to himself, this is neither the place nor the time regardless of how attracted he was to the girl, but he was willing to allow it. It is hard to think about that kind of thing when adrenaline is still flowing through you after nearly being killed, but there was something about Mary Jane that made John lose his senses. "Let me give you something to help you relax," she said, handing him a piece of chocolate.

"Chocolate is supposed to help me relax? How about lighting some candles and playing romantic music too," he said half-sarcastically.

"It's not *just* chocolate you goof. There is something in it that will help open your understanding. The chocolate is just there to mask the taste."

"So much for not taking candy from strangers," John said just before eating the piece of chocolate. The world suddenly seemed much bigger to John, and much smaller at the same time. He started to feel lighter. His lungs got cloudy again. He heard his voice as if it were far away, in a much lower pitch. "What did you give me?" he asked, as everything started to turn white. John could feel all of his energy unite. It was all being stored in this body that he was wearing. It connected with everything. What was this? There was a slight pressure in his forehead.

"All right John. Here comes the hard part," Mary Jane began. "Some of this is going to be difficult for you to understand. I pray that it will work. I need you to relax and let go while I explain what I can. First, the world is not as we see it. I already mentioned that time has already happened, it is all one, we see it all at once, not linearly like you do. That is just a mental block. It is one of the hardest things to overcome, and we don't have enough time to work on it now. The most important thing we need to focus on is you John. Well, not you as John, but you as what you really are. We are all part of one giant energy system. When they say energy cannot be created or destroyed they are right, but it can easily be relocated, manipulated, and connected. A long time ago we could manipulate it freely, but then something came along and blocked all access we had to control the universe. Someone decided it would be better if we didn't know anything about it. They wanted us to only see part of the picture and to struggle through life. That is where most people are. Stuck. It's like they are looking at a two-way mirror and only see one side of it. This knowledge started leaking out slowly into the world. It is impossible to contain something so universal. In places with suffering, it is strongest and easiest to see. You hear all kinds of stories of people lifting cars and doing impossible things. They are all possible. We just have to believe in it or the mind will stop us. The limits are of our own perception. The world we see is not the world that is really there. Are you starting to feel it John?"

John was feeling it. His thoughts seemed miles away, yet they were spoken clearly as they floated by. John watched them in some part of his existence. He could see the thoughts come and go, but it was like another person speaking them in his head. John could feel everything. He was finally seeing things for what they were. Here was this voice in front of him, coming from the beautiful girl with green hair. He knew the words even before she spoke them, as if the subtitles were ahead of the dialogue. As John let out his next breath (which seemed to take forever), he could see a glow of light dissipate in his exhalation. The questions his mind had for what all of this was, were stifled and passing by in the background. Everything felt right. Relaxed. Perfect. Content. No want or need for anything more.

"You look like you're enjoying it," said Mary Jane. "That's good. Now it's time for the harder part. You have to let go of everything you believe. Nothing here is real. All of it can be changed, altered, and adapted by you. You have to forget about science. There is no gravity. All of the laws we have been given were put there to hold us back. Nothing is the color that you see or even in the same place. You can see the entire history and future of everything, but I am getting ahead of myself. We need to start this simply. Hold out your hand." John lifted his arm, which seemed to no longer be an attachment of his body. The hand lifted and he watched as it went up, not feeling that it was part of him.

"Okay. Do you see any of the glowing?"

"My hands. Are they still mine?"

"Are they still whose, John? They are still part of a body, did they ever really belong to anyone? You see them as your hands, but they are no one's hands. There are no hands. There is no you. Everything is the same, it is all one big existence. I know it is hard to understand. The hand is as much mine as it is yours," she said. Mary Jane flexed her fingers and John saw his own fingers do the same. "Let go of your attachment. None of it is real," she said. John moved his fingers and watched as her fingers did the same. "Now you are getting it," she said, noticing her own fingers moving at his command. Somewhere in the universe John could see himself through her eyes, even though he was still there looking at her. A thought came by of what else he could do as her, but it passed by as quickly as it appeared, stifled by the no-mind state of the chocolate.

"Think of an object," said Mary Jane, "anything will do, but it has to be something you can hold in your hand. I want you to imagine that you are holding it. I want you to bring that object to your hand. Ignore anything that tells you it isn't possible." John could not do his own thinking at this point. He was beyond his own mind in existence. The answers were laid out before they were given for his mind to think. There was no John. In his hand appeared a small stuffed animal. It was a little tiger cat. John had never seen it before. "Why did you create that?" asked Mary Jane, backing up slightly. "How did you... know? John," she continued, "it really is you. I can see it."

The cat started to levitate in John's hand, a few inches above. It moved like a real animal, but as far as John's mind was concerned it was in his hand sitting still, as stuffed animals often do. John was beyond that at this point. He did not reject what was right in front of him.

"When I was a young girl, I had a stuffed cat just like this," said Mary Jane. "I took it with me everywhere, but one day I lost it. It seemed like some unseen force took it away from me. You brought it here John. That is the same cat I had as a little girl." Mary Jane looked down for a minute, trying to move past this because she didn't think John was ready to understand it, and because deep down she wasn't ready either. This was the first time he was being educated on the subject and already he had unknowingly done something that had a deeper meaning for her.

"What happened to your stuffed cat?" asked John, a question that came out of nothingness because it had to exist for the answer to follow. It wasn't John asking the question, and it wasn't the question that mattered, but the answer that it needed for the next thing to happen.

"I found it a few moments later, like it had been there all along." The cat disappeared from John's hand. At that moment a timer went off, beeping somewhere in existence (or perhaps non-existence). "We're running out of time... well... in this linear progression of it. It has already been four hours," said Mary Jane. She took out a large book. On the cover was one word written in big gold letters, "Apertambuxtion." "Everything you need to know is in here. Take this book." She handed it to him. As he touched it the book seemed to be shrinking, but it wasn't really changing in size, it was integrating with his hands. In a few seconds the book was gone, molding itself into John's energy. "The sections will open as you need them... I have faith in you. It is not going to be easy, and you are the only one who can do it." Again, the color started to disappear from the world. "Goodbye John. I will see you again when we are meant to. It is sooner than you know," she said, slowly fading away. The world went dark, and the next thing John knew, he woke up with a splitting headache in his own bed. Everything felt very tight and compressed. He had been stuffed into a limited space after having been the universe.

Chapter 3
Connecting

What had just happened? Was that a dream? John's thoughts were back to normal again. They were thoughts in John's head that belonged to him; he, the thinker, knew that they had come from him and nothing else. It was John's mind knowing that, taking comfort in it. There was still John beyond where he was only John, who knew the truth.

He got off the bed too quickly and stumbled a bit as there was disorientation, a ringing in his ears, and a flash of light. He let out a small, "agh" of agony, like it was the hangover from hell. His body felt tight, as if he couldn't fit inside of it. He was very squirmy, moving his body like it was new to him. John's limbs were sore and tingly, there was a sensation of something pressing on them from the inside. John looked at his clock and realized it was the middle of the day. How long had he been sleeping? How did he get back home? All viable questions that his mind would pass by while he was trying to organize his thoughts toward what he should do next. John took out his cellphone and found the number for the store. As the phone was ringing John wondered what he was going to say. How was he going to explain what had happened there? Did he even have a job anymore? There was a click as the line was opened on the other end and he heard the voice of his boss, "This is the general store downtown, Bob speaking."

"Bob," said John. "Are you all right?"

"Am I all right? What do you mean? Who is this?" asked Bob, even though he presumably recognized John's voice.

"It's John. What happened this morning? Should I come back into work?" asked John, even though he really didn't want to go back. He still had a leftover connection with the life he thought his earlier identification of John was supposed to be living.

"Nothing has really happened, it has been a slow morning. It's your day off John, I appreciate your commitment to the store and frankly didn't expect as much from you. We are fine here for today, stay home and relax," said his boss.

"Okay... yeah," said John, not understanding very much of this. Had he dreamed the whole thing? Wasn't he supposed to be working today? John said goodbye and hung up the phone. Did that really happen or had it really been a dream? John had never dreamed like that before.

"No. It wasn't a dream," came a voice from the bathroom. John walked over to the bathroom doorway and saw that no one was in there. But there was someone there. In the mirror. It was John. Not his reflection. It was him. He saw someone on the other side as if he was looking through a window at some kind of doppelganger who was a near perfect version of John himself. "Yes. It's me John, I am you. Even if you haven't gotten it yet," said the mirror version of John.

"How is this possible?" asked John, who was pretty confident that he was the one standing in the bathroom, looking at the mirror.

"This is pretty neat, huh? Once you get more in tune, I will be able to appear out of thin air, right next to you, and even interact physically! It's incredible. I am part of you

15

John, we are connected through all existence. You need to trust Mary Jane. She will be there to help you when you need her. I will be too John, but you need to trust yourself too, and I don't mean me. Forget everything you think you know. We are on to the first section of the book John," continued the mirror John. The words, "Section 1," appeared floating in the air, and the title right below it, "Connecting."

"Connecting," John said.

"You see it. Good," said the mirror image. "The first section is an introduction on feeling and connecting with everything. It is all there and you are part of it, but there is a blockage that we need to get past before you can do anything without eating the chocolate." John's head lifted slightly as he was hit with a small burst of energy, that came with the entire section of the book, word for word, flowing into his conscious mind. "You will get the new sections when you need them, and are ready for them. For now don't worry about the Masked Man finding you. We redirected your energy signal, so you should be safe for the duration of your training. It was great seeing myself again. Eventually you will be on this side of the mirror," said the mirror image before it faded into John's own reflection. John waved before the mirror and watched his own hand follow. The mirror was back to normal again. But was he? Who was the Masked Man that his mirror image had just mentioned? Did he mean the futuristic man? He wasn't wearing a mask last time they met.

Part 1 of this new book in his brain seemed to go slowly, as most books do. Too bad they can't jump right into the action, John thought to himself. He was glad, at least, that he didn't have to read twenty pages of introduction, acknowledgements, and notes from other authors before beginning, though he would have liked to see the table of contents. He imagined that it wouldn't make any sense at this point anyway, so there was no reason to skip ahead even if that was a possibility. Some parts of the section were fuzzy to him and others didn't seem to make sense at all, but he understood the overall message and instructions. It said something like, "John," (John thought it was interesting that the book even used his name, but was that really the strangest part of having a book directly absorbed into your head?).

"John, this book will provide you with…" blah blah blah boring part that continued for a little while, "the essentials that you need to know are as follows. Everybody has been programmed throughout their lives to be what they think they are now. It is a prison that we are led into since childhood. Most people accept it freely and hold on to the idea that what they are living is real. It is easier for people who never fit in to let go of the idea of themselves, something about it never sat right with them. They are the lucky ones because not belonging makes them question the illusion, and gives them a chance to break free. The main purpose of this section is to teach you to let go of what you have been taught is reality, and to instead connect with what really is. You may have experienced this before, when you had to look at something twice because the first time it seemed like it didn't register properly, or when you saw someone out of the corner of your eye, but turned to see nothing there. The truth is John, the second time you looked is when it didn't register properly. That feeling of dread that came over you in the second it took to look back was the real world seeping into an otherwise fantasy existence."

Whose voice was this, John wondered. Anytime he read a book it would be in his mind's voice, but this one sounded more authoritative like he was about to be given a mission by someone in a secret organization. The first section continued to describe some of the impossible events that occur in his world every day, but John had been convinced that there was something beyond what he had been living, well before the book started describing these situations. Next in the section came the instructions. Not all of the instructions were written, most were simply understood. It was as if they were telling John to do something as simple as tie his shoe when it was really a complex yoga posture that he would have never known before.

The section continued, "The essence of this system is to use control over what you have direct access to, in order to open pathways to archaic connections that human beings seldom use. When your pathways are open you will be more than John. You will connect with the greater universe. As long as you let this happen freely and openly, there will be nothing stopping you from the greatest of human achievements, from reading minds to bending the very fabric of space and time. Through this book you have been given the knowledge of how to perform the tasks needed for achieving this. For most people it would take a lifetime, or a thousand lifetimes, to study and learn these skills, yet alone perfect them, and connect with the greater universe. You may have noticed that you have been given the day off. That was our doing. You can use this time, and much more time than you think there is here, to advance to the next step. When you are ready, time will flow normally, but do not worry about this, as it is in our control and we are here to help you. Good luck John, it has been an honor talking to you." John thought that was a weird thing for a book to say, but with all of this talk of space and time not existing, it didn't really matter very much that he was being flattered by an inanimate object.

More so, he wondered who wrote the book, than why it seemed to be having a direct conversation with him. One thing he did know, it was time to get started.

The first thing John was supposed to do to open his mind was yoga and meditation. John was hesitant to do this because most of what he had been taught was negative toward other cultures and religions. John didn't like the idea of betraying his own beliefs, but he was open enough to give other ideas a chance before dismissing them without cause. The rules said he was supposed to be clean and pure when he did his practice, so he started by taking a shower. Truthfully, John felt silly for what he was going to attempt, and was using the shower as one more thing to put between him and this new and unusual activity. It was happening as it was supposed to. John's programming of who he thought he was had already started fighting against this process of opening.

After showering, John put on comfortable clothes and sat down cross-legged. He closed his eyes and sat there. His mind was doing a good job of being silent, he thought, not recognizing that it was broken by this thought. He waited. Nothing happened. "Ohmmmmmm," John said. He peeked from one eye, but everything was still normal. Nothing seemed to be happening. Then John remembered he was supposed to do some of the exercises before starting the meditation. If he had been paying attention to the thoughts in his head, John would have realized this was another distraction of his mind, but it was consequently leading him to the right place. His mind was buying time, but this was going to happen. The positions of his body were meant to open up energy pathways and allow everything to flow naturally. Some of them would have caused great pain for an inexperienced practitioner. Somehow John knew how to do the postures perfectly and without any great struggle. He did a swan dive forward then held the bottoms of his feet with his hands. He twisted his body both ways and lifted his knees close to his chest before swinging them in the air and holding them above his head. The changes in posture came with great ease as if John had been doing this for many lifetimes. His body moved as gracefully as someone doing the tango.

After an hour or so of rhythmic breathing and stretching, John could feel how his body had changed. Everything was tingling. He noticed every part of his body from the tips of his toes to the top of his head. He could feel parts of his body that he had never felt before. Inside and out. It wasn't as intense as it had been while he was eating the chocolate, but it seemed like he was going down the same path. At this point very few thoughts went through John's mind, and the ones that did received no attention. He had already entered the ideal brain state for meditation. They say every minute of practice is worth one hundred years of evolution. John had progressed many centuries already and was breaking the barrier between man and what most people would call God. The harder it seems for a person to meditate, the closer they are to breaking through if they made the effort.

John sat down cross-legged, this time in a position that would make most people cringe just to look at. He no longer witnessed his actions as the doer, but just as an observer. He felt the great hum coming from all existence including his own being. An outside observer, who was still stuck in their own mind, would have witnessed a person sitting there humming, not unlike bored schoolchildren in detention. John was discovering the universe, neigh, becoming the universe. The hours that he spent sitting there with and without himself were turned into an eternity. It was a timeless state. All of existence: being, observing, feeling, and connecting. When John finally stood up, it was already midnight and it was time to go to bed.

John lay in bed not knowing whether his eyes were open or closed, feeling parts of his brain and energy that he didn't think humans could feel. He connected with them and stimulated them, feeling his own control over how the neurons flowed and functioned. It wasn't until three hours later that John was in the state of sleep that most of us associate as normal. Even then, it was much deeper and more free from limitation. Upon waking, John didn't feel any different than usual, though he did feel very relaxed, and his mind didn't seem to have very much to say. There was a pleasant quietness that filled the space his thoughts had occupied for so long. Looking in the mirror, he was surprised to see himself there. It was the reflection of his body, but he had forgotten that he was someone inside of a body. Identification was slipping, just as the book had intended. Everything felt perfect. Every sensory experience, John witnessed uniquely. They seemed so beautiful. Seeing, hearing, feeling. John moved through the world slowly as if a visitor for the first time, taking in all there is in this world. Things were so interesting, but nobody took the time to notice it. It was all so... new. John didn't know it yet, but he had finished the first part of his journey.

Chapter 4
The Coffee Shop

One of John's frequent hangouts was a coffee shop a few blocks down the street from his house. He didn't exactly decide to go there so much as he felt himself being drawn there by an unknown force. As if he was a leaf being pulled by the wind. It was what he was supposed to do next, and he knew it. Whether or not he wanted to had no importance in the matter. Though he had connected with the universe, and could have driven with his eyes closed at this point, (though his mind would never let him) John walked instead, watching everything in slow motion. It seemed like John would reach light speed if he decided to start running, but there was no need because he could already see himself on every part of this journey, the whole experience of walking to the coffee shop had already happened, and he was watching it as if watching a movie he had already seen. It was all so familiar, so easy, so perfect.

John opened the door to the coffee shop at an angle, allowing someone with their hands full to walk through easily. There was no way he could have known someone was coming out at that very moment, but it had already happened and he was carrying out his part in it. As he was standing in line he heard a voice in front of him that said something like this, "Darn it, where did I put my keys."

John knew the answer. He put his hand on the shoulder of the woman in front of him and said, "In your left jacket pocket."

The woman checked there and found the keys. She gave John a wide-eyed look of distrust and kept quiet for the rest of the time she was in line. John heard her voice again, but her lips were not moving, "Now how did he know that. Lucky guess, I suppose. This guy had better not be following me or I'm going to smack him with my purse."

The emotions attached to it passed by John like an airplane in the sky up above. The passing feelings of other minds were lifetimes away from his consciousness. Everything was matter of fact. It just was. It existed. The meaning did not. Meaning is an attachment of the mind that creates suffering. John was still in a dreamy state of perfection, connected with things you and I may never be able to understand. When John got to the counter, he exchanged the usual pleasantries with the barista, "How are you today?" John said in a voice of utter bliss.

"Good, how are you," said the Barista, distracted by her attachment to the idea that she was a barista, and under pressure to do her job. She was miles away from coming close to discovering the truth that was overwhelming John.

"Perfect," John said, "I'll have a medium coffee, black, with no room... and a macchiato for the girl behind me." John had not looked behind him and couldn't possibly have known who was there, yet alone what drink they were going to order.

"And don't worry, your cat will be fine," he said, handing her his money: exact change and a dollar for the tip jar. The barista gave him a surprised look that contained partial confusion, and continued the transaction. She justified that John must have heard her talking about it earlier. Then John was struck. It is overwhelming to witness the perfection of the universe as it happens. He turned around to see the girl he had ordered for just as she started asking him how he knew what she wanted. A beautiful voice. He made eye contact with her and everything inside of him exploded. His connection to reality was coming back, though it had never left, he has simply connected with the other side in place of it. John was walking on the line of both worlds. He knew this girl. He had already seen her before.

"My name is," said the girl.

"Mary Jane," John whispered as she spoke. Her hair was dark, almost a shade of black. "Will you sit with me?" John asked her as they collected their drinks from the end of the counter.

"I suppose it would be rude of me not to," said Mary Jane. It was as though she didn't know who he was. John tilted his head slightly as most people do in interested confusion. It wasn't making sense to the logical mind part that was all John had until recently, but he still heard the answer from the other side speaking as well.

In the regular progression of time, this is the first time you meet. The world seemed to expand into infinity in John's mind. He was blown away by this revelation. Just yesterday a confident Mary Jane with green hair was telling him how to control the universe and today he is sitting having coffee with a shy girl who isn't sure if she should run away from this stranger. Luckily, the same force from the other side of existence was also in control of Mary Jane, allowing her to break her own social boundaries and have coffee with this cute, mind-reading stranger. It was the only way it could be.

If you think it didn't make sense to Mary Jane, remember how little sense all of this was making to John, who was worried about being late for work so recently. John had the feeling that he would be spending his future with this girl, and if he made one mistake he could ruin the course of history. Was that possible? It was a scary thought to his mind, but his connection to the other side knew that he could only do what he was meant to. Only what was meant to happen could happen. Control is part of the illusion.

"So are you some kind of psychic?" asked Mary Jane.

"Not exactly. I just started finding out about this myself... some crazy things have happened, and it is like there is a whole world out there, that is right in here, in all of us. Within you, without you. There is no more need to read minds because you are that mind as well as everything else in the universe, and you no longer have yourself to worry about," replied John.

"So tell me, what number I am thinking of." She wasn't entirely ready for this message. Her mind brought in this distraction. This challenge, to take her away from the truth.

"Ha ha, it doesn't work like that," said John, but his voice continued even though it wasn't him speaking, '27'. Now you are thinking of a black cat named Snuffles. The cold chimichanga you had from breakfast, that was left over from dinner with your parents. Hawaii. You already know this. You feel it too. You have been waiting for me to take you out of it. Now you are thinking of..." John's voice was cut off as Mary Jane kissed him. He wasn't sure if it was to shut him up or because her world had just changed. Everybody reacts differently to being shown the other side. John was the catalyst. Had he really done anything?

"I knew it. Everyone I know thinks I am crazy. I can't believe you found me and we can get out of all of this."

"I feel like you found me," replied John, "and like I said, I just started this myself, so I don't really know what to do next. Whatever needs to happen just kind of happens when it is meant to if you are open to it."

"You mean, our meeting was not a coincidence... but the only way it could have been?"

"Yeah, exactly like that. The way it had to be. I don't think we can do anything that we are not supposed to do. I can't explain where that feeling is coming from, but it has been with me since this started. Before I felt trapped in a life that wasn't mine, and now it's like I really am trapped, except it's in a life that I want to be a part of." John took a sip of some of the best coffee in the world right before everything went wrong.

Mary Jane was the first one to notice it. "John, nobody is moving." She was connecting. John knew he hadn't mentioned his name to her yet, it had to be the other side pushing it's way through. More importantly, she was right. It wasn't that nobody was moving, it was that they were frozen. One person in mid step, another just about to finish sipping his coffee. In this silence their voices sounded like they were on a stereo. "Are you doing this?" she asked. John heard the old fashioned bell ring as someone opened the door to the coffee shop. It was the Futuristic Man from before, followed by someone else wearing a mask. John could tell from their demeanor that the man in the mask was in charge. This must be who Mirror John had mentioned earlier. The man pushed the door closed behind them slowly, as if it had been opened underwater.

"You can't escape from us John. We want to help you," said the Masked Man. "You are going to come with us whether you want to or not."

"Your man tried to kill me, why would I go anywhere with you?" asked John, trying to think of one of his new skills that would get them out of this situation.

"Your whole world is changing John. You know that as well as I do. I know how overwhelming it can be, everything probably seems great right now, but that will change in time. You are going to be completely alienated from your whole world, John, why would you want that? I want to help you get back to your normal life, where everything makes sense. Back to the things you love and the people who like you just the way you are. This new world you are connecting with is dangerous and who knows what will happen if you keep doing these things? You could really hurt someone." said the Masked Man.

"You call that living? Being a slave? A prisoner? Stuck in a world molded with restrictions that are meant for weaker beings. What would make anyone want to hide themselves from this? This is what freedom really is. No more restrictions." John replied.

"John, people aren't ready for this. That is why they created the restrictions for themselves. Look how crazy they get over insignificant things, what would happen if they knew about the big ones? It would be chaos. They would feel lost and meaningless, completely helpless. In their world they are accomplishing something meaningful. They have things to be hopeful for and to achieve. They thrive on their need for creation and meaning. They would be lost without it."

"It should be their choice," said John, "plenty of people would rather be free if they knew what it meant."

"It is no longer a choice for them. It was their decision. People have already created their reality, and that is where they have to live. You either know it or you don't. These people need the limits they impose upon themselves so they can feel comfortable. They love feeling like they have control. It isn't up to us to help them out of it. Once you have seen the truth, there is no going back, and you would be responsible for all of the people who were stuck in this missing their friends, family, and everything that made them who they were before you imposed your 'help' upon them. They love being in their cages. It is comforting to them. People don't want to lose themselves, John, that is their biggest, most important possession, it's their biggest attachment! They can't imagine a world where they don't exist, even when they are living in it!"

The Futuristic Man was startled by Mary Jane who wasn't supposed to be moving. "There is someone else here," he said.

The Masked Man said, "Wait, no!" but the Futuristic Man had already unleashed a ball of energy right toward Mary Jane. John dove in front of it to protect her. This was going to hurt. Being struck by the ball of energy John completely evaporated and there was nothing left of him in the coffee shop. "Now look what you've done!" yelled the Masked Man. Anyone with at least one eye or some sort of emotional perception would tell you there was a look of regret on the Futuristic Man's face, and a look of horror on Mary Jane's. His head hung low and he cowered before his superior. "Let's go," said the Masked Man, as he opened the door to the outside.

"What about her?" asked the Futuristic Man gesturing toward Mary Jane.

"She found her way here, she can find her way out," replied the Masked Man, shutting the door behind them. Mary Jane ran toward the door and tried to open it, but she couldn't get it to budge. The world was frozen. She started to panic as she made her way back to the table where she and John were drinking coffee minutes ago.

"John," she spoke his name through tears, causing her emotions to cry out even further. She was able to take a sip of her macchiato, which apparently hadn't been frozen either. There must have been a bubble around the table where she and John were sitting, of things that could still move after time stopped. A fate worse than death, it seemed Mary Jane was going to be stuck here forever. Would she get older? Would she ever have to go to the bathroom? All of these thoughts and more were whirling through her head when she noticed something that hadn't been there before. She started to laugh through her tears even though her conscious mind didn't know why. There was a book on the table in front of her. A large book with big gold letters on it that read, "Apertambuxtion."

Chapter 5
Space

Things felt slow as John dove in front of this dark-haired Mary Jane he had just met, to save her from the incoming electrical blast. Was it electricity? It was some kind of energy. Did other energy act that differently from the way electricity does? At a base level at least. It wasn't that important because John was going to see how it would act on him right at this moment. He was struck in the chest with the energy. He felt it spread out over his whole body, covering his skin and then pulling inward to every last bit of him. What we observed as John being disintegrated at that very moment, John experienced as light, heat, and then darkness. After a whole lot of pain, there was nothing left, but John was still there. He wasn't there in the sense that you and I would see him there, and talk to this person who is in the room with us. In fact he wasn't in the room at all. He didn't know where he was and there was no body for him to be in either. A bodiless existence of floating in darkness. Did he still exist? There has to be some way out of this, John thought. Was he thinking? There was no body or brain, who was left to be thinking?

Then he heard Mary Jane's voice. First he heard his name through her crying, then he heard a single word that changed everything. "Apertambuxtion," said Mary Jane, as she read the cover of the book.

There was a bright flash in John's world and he found himself back in his body. He was on the beach again looking out toward the ocean. He gasped air into his newfound lungs. His whole body ached, where had it been? John was afraid to think about it. Was it a new body? They say your body completely regenerates itself in a number of years anyway, and was it ever really his anyway? The man with the dark goatee again walked forward toward John with his hands held in prayer posture. He opened them toward John as he began to talk. "Ahh, you are back. Excellent. We have more time now. You are ready for the next section of the book."

"Where is Mary Jane?" asked John, as if this man would know anything about it. Fortunately he did.

"She is fine, John. They left her there after you were... um... disappeared so to speak. She is safe for now. I am sorry to say we can't do anything to help her right now. We have to work on you. But I am getting ahead of myself. We have never been properly introduced. My name is Howard."

"We have to get her out of there," said John.

"I understand how you feel, John, but there is nothing we can do from here. We have to continue your training."

"Where exactly is here?"

"Ha! Right to the point. Most people would call it another dimension. I like to call it Hawaii. As you can see there is no one else here. It is not by any means actually Hawaii. It just reminds me of a time passed when I was younger and things hadn't changed. I live here, John. They won't let me leave this place, and I am sure I would be killed if I did. I knew someone would come one day who could help me, and likewise someone I could help as well. You will notice time is different here, in that it is virtually non-existent. Everything seems to be happening normally, but nothing really goes on. The sun is always shining and we are never hungry, thirsty, or tired. It is very convenient really, for productivity and all... if there was anything to do."

"Do you know how long you have been here? I mean in real time." asked John, not sure if it was an appropriate question.

"It's okay. I have been here for what would be considered many years, but time isn't real even when it does pass, John. I don't know any specific number of years. I lost count because I never had anything to use to keep track. The daylight never changes, and I have no watch. It might not tick here, even if I did have one. I can only guess how long it has been, but for all intents and purposes it is an eternity, and that eternity continues this very moment. But we are not here to talk about me, John. We are here to get you ready for the next leap." John wasn't sure if he could trust the man, but remembered he had been saved earlier by Howard, and that he didn't have any other choice as long as he was there.

"Are you ready for the next section?" asked Howard. "It is titled, Space." Words appeared in front of John, and moved with his vision, "Section 2, Space." The information for this section flowed into John's mind, still in a voice that was not his. He imagined the feeling was similar to being conscious during a seizure.

This is what John remembers of Section 2: "There are two types of space. Inner space and outer space. Most people in the world you were occupying are familiar only with the latter. Outer space was deemed more important, as it was something that they could perceive through sight and sense. Inner space could never be captured or observed in a worldly fashion. People have been taught to overlook how deep one can go into inner space, in exchange for material gratification and a constant search for something they can never hold on to. They are looking in the wrong place. They are looking without, instead of within. Everything is inside. There is no outer space. It is all illusion. An idea. A creation, projection, and reflection of the mind. The world, all of everything, is inside of you."

"What we think that we see in this world is all a reflection of our inner self. Every color, every texture, every perception, is defined by our own interpretation. Have you ever hurt yourself and not felt the pain until you looked at it? Before the mind chose its interpretation, there was no reaction involved, but when it decided what it was seeing, and interpreted what that meant, then the meaning became real, and physical pain was felt. This is why we are taught to meditate with our eyes closed. The biggest misinterpretation of existence comes from perception of that world through sight. As a species we have grown to depend most on this one sense, while the others are left in the background. That is why the other senses are easier to surpass. They have never been as prominent and depended upon."

"As we discussed earlier, these senses are fallible. Sometimes the real world seeps through and we are frightened until the mind blocks it, ignores it, or rationalizes it. Fortunately, we were made with the ability to shut off sight with very little effort. We can close our eyes to ignore the blatant illusion of vision, and go in to our inner selves through stillness, silence, and sightlessness. Space appears to be all around us in everything we see and touch, but in reality there is no space at all. Space is another part of the illusion that this world uses to imprison us, but it had to exist for our physical bodies to be there and act as containers. That is where the idea of separation came in. Once we reach our inner selves, we can see past the illusion of space, and the idea that we are the body we occupy, thereby allowing our true selves to move about freely. With enough practice, you can even take your physical body with you as you move freely through what appears to be space. With the guidance of Howard, and this book, you will be able to transport yourself through space in a way that will get you back to your world." I just want to get back to Mary Jane, thought John.

"We will have to start small John," said Howard, somehow knowing the book had just finished what it was saying. Could he hear it too? "First show me the postures you have learned, then enter into the meditative state. To start, you must feel and know the space around you while you are meditating. This will give you a starting point for the space you currently appear to be occupying, as well as the idea of distance around it. From there you will start connecting with other spaces and planes. They are infinite in number. You will start to see them, hear them, and feel them. Then we will work on moving you through them, both with and without your body."

It seemed like a heavy load to bear. John's mind didn't think what he was about to attempt was possible, but John remembered to keep his mind at bay and let go of any association with what is and is not possible. The biggest thing that holds you back is what you believe. He had already traveled a few places and distances without meaning to, so he knew that it was possible whether he believed it or not. The innate ability was already there. John went through the physical postures again, each time getting a nod of approval from Howard. After he had completed the same postures as last time, new ones were unlocked to his mind. He completed them as well. They were coming as he needed them and when he was ready for them. John didn't feel like he was the one controlling his body anymore. The postures were happening on their own and his body was following them as if they had been done a thousand times before. He dared not think about what could happen if he did some of them wrong. Whether he hyper-extended his leg, broke a bone, or even worse ended up moving only half of his body through space, while leaving the other half behind. Was it possible to get separated from his body? Forever?

"JOHN." Howard scolded him. "There is no body to get lost from. It is an illusion. All part of nonexistent space that people believe in. You must understand that you and your body are no more a part of space than anything else that you perceive, including the space itself. It is easy once you understand that none of it is real." John nodded, got into his meditation posture (cross-legged), and closed his eyes. He started to hum. John flowed through the process with ease. He began as Howard said, noticing the space around him. The amount of time it took could not be measured because of the eternal plane John was inhabiting. As well, it could only take as long as it needed, and wouldn't happen a second before. If you wonder what this is like, close your eyes and imagine knowing every square inch of the space around you as well as the objects occupying them. Know it without using your senses.

Everything felt lighter when John left his body. Weightlessness. Well, *he* didn't leave his body, there was no John in this place where he seemed to be, separate from his body. It was beyond John. A connection to everything. John was sure that there was no visible apparition of himself, but he was there outside of his body looking in all directions. There was no one-directional set of eyes John was using, like he normally would. He saw his body from all sides, and out into the distance all around. All at the same time. He could see Howard's body sitting there in silence as well. Then he noticed Howard's energy floating outside of his body as well. It did not take on the same appearance as Howard's body, but somehow John innately knew it was him. It was like he didn't have to know. The same way you know which loved one is appearing in your dream, even if you don't see their face. "Aha," communicated Howard's energy, "Excellent. Your progress is fantastic. Now we will travel. Imagine yourself in a comfortable spot, somewhere you are familiar with, and bring us both there."

Starting to understand, John did not do anything or try to bring them anywhere, he simply felt it, and knew that it was. Not a moment later, he was in his bedroom. He could see everything. The clock ticking away slowly, cars passing outside. "Very good," said Howard's energy, who had come with John to this new location. "Your progress is outstanding. Now we will begin interacting. Try to pick up the cup on that nightstand." John tried, but could not even move in this space. He was not really there. It was just a connection with the space. There was no body, no hand to pick up the mug, and nobody to walk over to it. "You are here, but you are not really here," said Howard. "John, let go of the beach, and where you think you are. Understand that you are nowhere and that it is nothing new, you were never anywhere, and you never can be. This is just where you are perceiving at this moment. You must know you are here in this space, use the old belief that you had that this exists, and it will allow you to be a part of it. Feel yourself standing over the table, picking up the mug." This time John could see the time passing, the clock on his wall laughing. This isn't exactly easy, he thought to the clock snarkily. John tried very hard to connect to being in the bedroom, but it didn't work. Then he felt it come on it's own. He saw his own hand lifting the mug, and the mug was lifted. He let out a laugh, which broke his concentration, and the cup fell to the ground. Anyone present in the room would have heard the laugh which had also broken through, but shrugged it off as there was clearly no one else there. As for the floating cup, you just might start believing in ghosts if you had seen it. This was going to take a lot of practice.

Chapter 6
Crossing Over

Mary Jane lifted the cover of the book in front of her. "Apertambuxtion," she said. Upon touching the book, it followed the same process of integrating with her mind as it had with John. Mary Jane saw a window to another plane open in front of her, like a television screen floating in mid air. She saw John on the other side. He was sitting on a beach meditating. "John!" she called out to the image, but nothing happened. The image in the window changed again, this time to herself, but not in the coffee shop. The image of Mary Jane in the window had green hair and started speaking to her, "You found the book... well, maybe the book found you. All of this will make sense, I promise. Right now you have to trust me that it will be okay. John is all right and he is trying to get to you. I need you to open a window here that will allow a connection between the two of you so that you can be taken out. It is not as simple as you have just seen. That was only a picture of what is there, not a doorway. Even with the connection, you have to find a way out of this frozen space and back into the normal passage of time that John is occupying."

"How am I going to do that?" asked the coffee shop Mary Jane.

"You have to have faith. Just seeing that I am here now proves that it works. Read through the book and it will give you everything you need when you are ready," said the image of Mary Jane, before fading away into nothingness. Mary Jane wasn't sure how to start reading a book that had now disappeared, but her thought was interrupted with the answer. In the middle of the coffee shop, words appeared in front of her, "Section 1, Connecting." Mary Jane felt all of the information from the section expand in her mind and knew all of it at once. It was incredible to know so much, so fast. She started doing the physical postures and then sat on the table cross-legged, ready to start meditating.

Focus on opening a doorway, she thought to herself.

She heard John's voice, "This isn't exactly easy," followed shortly by a laugh. Mary Jane smiled and opened her eyes breaking the connection. Frustrated with herself, she closed her eyes again, and started to feel the connection. Mary Jane could see herself sitting in the coffee shop. The people started moving. She could see all of it around her, but as soon as the movement started, her body disappeared. She was stuck in that moment, even though she was connecting with the passage of time. It wasn't fair. She heard John call to her, "Mary Jane!" Then out of nowhere she saw John appear. He looked around for her, by the table where they had been sitting.

"I'm right here John!" she said to him. "Help me!" John looked up as if he heard her speak.

"Take my hand," he said. Mary Jane in her energy form thought of what it would be like to hug him right now, to get back to the world she was accustomed to. She could feel her hand in his. Then something happened. She felt herself falling, being pulled through the fabric of the universe.

"She is reaching out to us," said Howard's energy to John. They were both still in his bedroom, observing the broken cup that had been dropped. "You need to go to the coffee shop, John, but I can't go with you. Even in this energy form I should not have left the beach, but it was necessary. Go on to the coffee shop and get her back John," was the last thing John heard from Howard's energy before it disappeared.

John saw all of the places he could go. He could stay in the bedroom, go back to the beach, or move on to the coffee shop. Mary Jane was waiting for him. He focused on the coffee shop, and in no time was a form of floating energy right by the table with his still warm cup of coffee but his body was not there and neither was Mary Jane. The people were moving, he could see steam rising from the cup. He did not understand how everybody could be so calm in carrying out their coffee orders when something so transcendental was happening. He thought about sipping his cup of coffee then called out, trying to connect with wherever it was that Mary Jane had gone, "Mary Jane!" He felt himself being pulled and found his physical place in this perceived space.

John's vision was suddenly very limited, he could no longer see the universe, he could only see out of his own eyes which were in his own body that had been brought to the coffee shop. He held out his hand as he heard her voice, "I'm right here, John!" John held out his hand connecting with the space and time around him. John could feel her energy in the coffee shop. He knew she was there somewhere, he just had to find a way to bring her back.

"Take my hand," said John, hoping she could reach back from the other side. His hand was starting to disappear from the tips of his fingers upward as he reached his hand out toward where she had been. People were staring at him at this point wondering what was going on. Then it happened. John felt her hand in his, closed his eyes, and pulled. In a second, he was knocked back onto the floor as Mary Jane flew out of nothingness toward him. She landed on top of him where they were both filled with a sense of relief and closeness.

Their energy mingled as their connection to the other side made them one. She kissed him gently on the lips and said, "You found me."

"How could I go on without you?" he asked her. It was a strange sight to see the two of them on the floor together in the middle of the coffee shop but most of the minds around them had already placed Mary Jane in the coffee shop for all of the time she had been missing. They must have just been looking away if they remembered her not being there, as they could clearly see her now, she must have been there all along.

Chapter 7
The Flying Woman

Sitting back at the table, drinking their coffee, John and Mary Jane looked at each other, waiting to see who would speak first. They were both in a state of awe at what had happened, but they were also filled with relief at being reunited, and having gotten out of whatever dimensions it was they had been stuck in. Tension was high. Eventually Mary Jane spoke, "What do we do now?"

"We keep following the book." He was as much in the dark about all of this as she was. They were both following a path that neither of them had planned or understood, yet it always seemed to provide them with the right answer. They decided to go back to John's place and keep practicing.

It was much easier for both of them to do the postures and meditate with someone of like-mind present. John and Mary Jane frequently met in meditation, in an energy state. They seemed to gravitate toward each other no matter what plane they were on. Their connection to each other was as great as their connection to the other side.

"John, would you like me with green hair?" Mary Jane asked.

"I would like you with no hair," he said. They carried on in this fashion, flirting with each other in between being on the other side. Neither of them were quite sure what to do next because the book had not yet opened the next section to their minds. Mary Jane was struggling with the second section of the book, while John was patiently continuing his meditations, waiting to move on. It can only come when you are ready. While in meditation, John came to himself once again. This time it wasn't in the mirror, it was a physical appearance of John in the room with him. Mary Jane saw it as well.

"Is that you?" she asked him.

John, who was meditating, replied from a deeper place, "You can see him too? Good. It is me. He has been guiding me along this path. Or himself, I should say. In the end there is no you or me or him, it is all the same thing, all one."

Alternate John started to speak to them, "You have both gone a long way already, and there is still much to learn. I remembered that this was a particularly difficult part of the path, and realized that I was the reason that you get through this. John, don't forget to come back here and help yourself, like I am doing now. I am you from what you would call the future, but of course, it is a place inside of you as well. There is no time. The next step on your journey is to find people like both of you. They are out there. Some will be easier to find than others. They will be in many different places, both on this journey, and in the world. If you meditate and connect, you will be drawn to these people, and they will be able to help you open the next part of the book. Any time you feel stuck, seek out those who are like you, and listen to what they tell you. That is all I remember saying to myself, good luck to both of you." The image of alternate John disappeared as quickly as it came.

"I don't even know where to begin," said Mary Jane.

"We have to concentrate and the answer will come to us. We will be drawn to it. There is nothing to worry about. Even if we took the first step today and didn't know where we were going then we would still get where we needed to be. It is how the connection works," replied John.

They both continued meditating and a bit later spoke the same word at the same time as the word was brought forth from the other side into their minds, "Arches."

"What is Arches?" asked John, not particularly to anybody, but Mary Jane was listening.

"Let's look online." They turned on John's computer and John drew a blank once again at his password. Then he remembered it was the same as the title of the book. That couldn't have been a coincidence. The word had been with him all along even though he had never seen the book before. He dared not speak the word for he knew not what would happen if he said it aloud. Mary Jane couldn't help but notice what he was typing.

"Did you get the book after you used that as your password?" asked Mary Jane.

"No, it has been with me all along."

"John, do you think that you..." Mary Jane trailed off.

"No, it couldn't have been. Aha, here it is. Arches National Park." It was the first entry to appear on the search engine. Well, it was actually the whole first page on the search engine, and the next Arches was a French paper company, and that didn't seem to make any sense even though they had a really cool website. John made a note to himself to get paper from Arches one day because it seemed like the pinnacle of luxury and fine quality. It had never occurred to John that paper could be so snobby, but he liked the idea of holding soft velvety paper with a nice texture. "It must be this national park," said John, "I guess we're going to Utah."

"Do you think the person we're trying to find is Mormon?"

"Ha. I doubt it. Although... it seems anyone of any religion could stumble upon the truth... you know what I mean? Religions are just the beginning; they are a method we use in an effort to connect, but they always have too many restrictions to really get to the other side. Religions often have the right message somewhere in them, but always the wrong practice. We don't pay enough attention in religion to really open up the connection," said John matter-of-factly.

"I guess that makes sense," said Mary Jane. "I mean, my family is very religious, but they are so disconnected from anything that they could gain from their practice. They use it as a background to justify and live with the things they do wrong. They just use it to feel better about themselves. If anything, it is strengthening their disconnect to the other side."

"Should we just teleport ourselves there?" asked John.

"I don't think I'm ready for that," said Mary Jane, "not after being stuck in timelessness..."

"All right, I guess we're driving." There were three different paths for drive to the Arches National Park. One of them took eight hours, one of them seven hours, and the path they chose would take six hours and twenty five minutes, according to the internet.

"We have to stop by to see my parents before we go. They have been overprotective ever since my uncle disappeared. It would kill them if anything happened to me."

"I never knew my parents. My dad died when I was young and my mom went crazy. I tried to visit her once when I was older, but she was afraid of me. I think she thought I was somebody else. I kept trying to tell her it was me, her son."

"That's terrible. I'm so sorry," said Mary Jane giving him a hug, and a solemn, listless expression.

John packed everything he would need for the trip. They stopped by Mary Jane's apartment on the way so she could pack as well. The next thing John knew he was sitting on a couch next to Mary Jane listening to her talking to her parents about the trip she would be taking.

"Don't be too descriptive," John said to her in his mind. "They won't believe anything about connecting and the other side." Mary Jane acted as if she heard what he said. Maybe she had, or maybe she had come to that conclusion on her own. She told her parents she was going to take a few days away for a vacation. She told them she knew John for a while already, (which was partially true because of their connection) so that they wouldn't be worried about her leaving the state with someone she met so recently on this plane.

"He seems to be a nice young man. In fact, he looks so much like someone I used to know. Make sure to be safe," said her father. He paused for a moment and then continued on with fatherly advice, "Don't drive in the dark. Stop to sleep when you need rest. Don't talk to strangers or trust anyone who has a flat tire. Don't pick up hitchhikers or drive over the speed limit. Make sure you have enough gas."

"Oh Dad, I'll be fine. I know how to take care of myself," said Mary Jane.

"You know I love you sweetie, and if anything happened to you I wouldn't forgive myself. After your uncle disappeared... well you know," her Dad replied. Everyone knew he felt responsible for it. "You take care of her John, she is one in a million." John already knew that. John felt a connection with her that even he couldn't fully understand.

Before they knew it, they were driving through Moab. "Was it named after the Mother of All Bombs," John wondered. "If not, did they have the name before or after nukes were invented?" They made it to Arches National Park. "So now what do we do?"

"I guess we go hike and see if we find anyone." The answer became more obvious when they were a few steps into the forest and started to feel the vibration.

"Do you feel that?" said John. "There is a connection here to the other side." They followed the vibration through the beautiful landscape, taking time to enjoy the serenity and beauty of the land. In time they came upon a girl who appeared to be in her thirties sitting cross-legged under one of the arches that the park had been so aptly named after. There was nothing out of the ordinary about this girl beside the vibrations that John and Mary Jane felt emanating from her. That, and she was floating a foot off the ground.

"I am Mariela," said the girl. "From Bulgaria."

"This is Mary Jane, and I am John," said John. "We have come a long way to find you."

"You have come a long way, but you have not moved at all. This space is not real. That is why I sit here three feet off the ground enjoying my forest. Do you like it, by the way? I created it for my own enjoyment, and that of all who come to see it," said Mariela.

"It is beautiful," said Mary Jane.

"Yes, quite extraordinary," said John.

"It is nothing," replied Mariela. "It is not even real, just another part of the illusion. Pay no attention to it."

"How have you been here so long without being noticed?" asked John.

"Most of the people who come up here can't see it," replied Mariela. "Their minds won't allow it. They see me sitting on the ground and they pay no attention. The mind is so strong that it will create it's own reality from what it wants to believe, even when it is so clear there is nothing between me and the ground. But you have to understand, there is no ground, and there is no me to be floating above it. The rules of gravity were created by the mind, as well as space and time." Mariela floated free form, no longer cross-legged, to Mary Jane, and whispered in her ear, "He is a cute one, isn't he? You are lucky to have him. I had someone close to me many lifetimes ago. In this incarnation I do not need anyone, but it is still something to appreciate for those days when you are feeling really stuck in this world." Mary Jane blushed at the mention of John. She wouldn't be able to hide their connection from anyone. "I don't have anything else to tell you," stated Mariela to both of them. "But then again, I never do or did in the first place. What needs to be said will be said whether we intend upon it or not. It is never us saying it. The words are there, they just need someone to go through in order to be heard. Let go of the idea that the words you speak are your words, and you speaking them. Ah, here come the words now."

"The next thing you have to do is find The Cleaner. He has been through much suffering, and it has helped him to connect with the other side, even if he is not aware of it. He can be found back where you came from. You already have the word John, and you can use it however you would like. The most important thing I can tell you is not to hold on too tightly. The word is just another method. The result comes from within you, not from the word itself. As long as you believe, then you can do anything and get the same result. Once you get there, you will be able to say anything, even Rhinoceroses, or chocolate cake, and the result will be the same as if you used the real word. Understand that I do not speak it for your benefit. Now I must go back to my full meditation, call me any time if you need me, and I will appear. Now, I will send you on your way."

"But what about..." John started, but instantly found himself, and Mary Jane standing next to their car back at his house. They both went inside and John went to the fridge to see what there was to eat, while Mary Jane sat on the couch wondering how they were going to find The Cleaner.

"Do you want anything to eat?" asked John. Neither of them were particularly hungry but it seemed like forever since their last meal. In a way, the six hour car ride was less tiring than being teleported back home. They still didn't know how the energy for it worked.

"Sure, whatever you're having," she replied.

John made a pot of rice with vegetables and spices for them to eat while they were thinking about what to do next.

"Do you think it's safe to stay here?" Mary Jane asked.

"When I saw myself in the mirror... was it yesterday? When I saw myself, he said that he was blocking my energy signal so they shouldn't be able to find me. But that was before the coffee shop... I assume you're protected too. They didn't seem to pay any attention to you last time... and for all they know you are still stuck in between time and I am disintegrated. To be honest they could probably find us at any time in any place... but I don't think they will be able to as long as they are not supposed to, if that makes any sense at all. It seems like the story has already been written, and we are living it out now."

"That isn't very comforting, but I know what you mean," replied Mary Jane. "So I guess the next step will be here when we are ready, according to everything we have heard."

"Do you think we should start looking for someone else instead of The Cleaner?" asked John, thinking aloud.

"Well it's not like he is just going to come to us..." Mary Jane said. Then she was interrupted by a knock at the door.

Chapter 8
The Cleaner

KNOCK KNOCK KNOCK. There was a knock at the door. It was a confident and sound knock. It could be just about anyone at this point, but John and Mary Jane were not oblivious to the coincidence it would be if they had just been talking about him and he was at the door. For all they knew it could be the Masked Man coming to kill them both, or the girl from the national park asking for a ride to Utah.

John opened the door slowly to reveal a tall man with dark hair in his mid forties. The man was wearing a suit and a red bow tie. It was a look that was easy to identify with, for most business people, and those who are weary to trust strangers. His smile and demeanor drew you in, like he had been friends with you for years, and you wanted to be friends with him too. "Hi, my name is Jeff, I am the owner of Grime Fighters cleaning service. I already serve many local businesses, and a few of your neighbors. I am stopping by to see if you might be in need of our services. Working men like yourself shouldn't be wasting their time cleaning when they have much more important money making opportunities available." He didn't discriminate based on John's age, and gave his pitch with confidence.

John gave him a blank look, and looked back at Mary Jane. "Will you come in and join us for a cup of coffee?"

"Yes. I can do a quick look around and give you an estimate on how much it would be to clean your home," replied Jeff. As they were gathering around the kitchen table, Jeff's phone rang. "Ugh, it's my fan club. I am so sorry, I have to take this, it will only be a second, I promise," he told them, walking a few feet away.

"Do you think he's The Cleaner?" asked Mary Jane.

"Who else could it be… it's like the universe knows… it is with us all the time, the connection," John told her. Jeff finished his phone call and came back to the table. "Are you The Cleaner?" John asked.

Jeff laughed, "Ha, well some people do call me that. So you have heard of me? That's great. Then you know my skills are excellent, we are fully licensed, bonded, and insured, and all of our clients are more than satisfied with the job we do."

"We don't need you to do any cleaning," said John.

"The people who need it most don't know that they do. Why did you invite me in if you didn't think I could help you? I am a very busy man, I cannot just stay here entertaining you. I am afraid I am going to have to leave," said Jeff, clearly agitated.

Jeff was all the way to the front door before he stopped in his footsteps when John spoke, "Axton." Mary Jane gave him a strange look, trying to understand. He gave her a quick glance, trying to tell her that it came from the other side.

"Where did you hear that name, who have you been talking to?" asked Jeff.

"Then it is you isn't it. You are The Cleaner," said John.

"I'm afraid I don't like being at a disadvantage, tell me what this is about or I am leaving," The Cleaner said shortly.

"Mariela sent us to find you… or be found it seems. We have been connecting with the other side, and there is this book that is teaching us all different ways to be a part of everything. We are learning them so that we will be able to compete with this strange guy with spiked hair, and his boss who wears a mask. They are trying to keep people from realizing the truth. We were sent to find others like us, who would be able to give us advice and guidance," John explained.

"I don't know how I am supposed to help you, it means nothing to me. The whole world. It is all just energy in motion. I am doing my part, and have to hope that makes a difference," replied The Cleaner.

"We met you for a reason. There has to be some way that you have been connecting with the universe. Mariela said you experienced great pain and it acted as a doorway to the other side. Have you done anything that feels like it isn't part of this world?" asked John.

Jeff, The Cleaner, paused for a moment to consider whether or not he should open up to these strangers, but the decision seemed to be made for him. "Now that I think about it, there is one thing. It is not something I have shared with anyone before. If I tell you, then you have to promise you will do something for me in return."

"We will do anything we can to help you," said Mary Jane.

"I need you to find someone for me, and make sure he is okay," replied The Cleaner.

"Well, we might be able to with some luck," said John. "But why ask us instead of a private detective?"

"Because he is no longer in this world," said The Cleaner, no longer holding up his facade of liveliness and excitement. "I need you to find my son, Axton. He died when he was young, and it has left me an empty shell. I live just to keep working, and hoping that I will make a difference. If you can do this for me, it will mean the world to me."

"We will do our best," said John. "It shouldn't be that difficult if we continue on our path at this rate. What is it that you can tell us?"

"Thank you," he said. "You don't know how much it would mean to me just to know that he was all right, wherever it is that he is. What I practice came to me on my own, no one taught me. It is a way of going out by going in. I do it while I lay in bed at night, waiting to fall asleep, but you can do it while you are meditating if you wish. Really, you can do it anywhere, at anytime, connect with the other side I mean. I lay still and I feel my whole body, my very existence. I label every part of it, associate with it and dissociate with it. This is my leg, this is not my leg. I let go of my body, and identification, and then I go through the universe. I fly through the stars and galaxies at light speed, seeing and feeling everything. When I do this it builds up energy, and gives me access to all of existence. It gives me a great charge, the power of a million suns, the energy to do this every day with such excitement, and keep going on day after day, living with this weight on my shoulders. If you are ever feeling defeated, or as if you just don't want to go on anymore, connect with this by leaving your body and powering up. That is all I can tell you. Here is my card, let me know when you find him."

"Thank you," said John taking the business card. 'Officer Jeff Barnes, Grime Fighters,' it said, 'Don't let grime go unpunished,' followed by contact information.

"Now if you'll excuse me I have to go," said Jeff. "There are homes that need to be cleaned." Jeff let himself out through the front door, while John and Mary Jane sat there contemplating what they had just heard. They needed a moment to let it sink in.

They both decided it would be a good idea to try out this new lesson. They did some of the postures and breathing exercises, before sitting down to meditate. They started as he said, feeling every part of their existence, and then dissociating from it. Everything felt a lot lighter, like a weight had been lifted. Without being so deep into the mind they were free of the pressure that is created on this plane. Anyone practicing similar techniques would note that Mary Jane was starting to emit a white light from her being. John was having a harder time than she was with this practice. He was flying through the stars, feeling incredible energy, but he was not ready for it. John was still there while he was doing this, and had not let go of his mind or attachment. He struggled to control it, and was lost in flight throughout the universe. Just as he was about to scream, he found himself back in his body and there was a bright flash of light from his hands followed by a crashing noise that was unmistakably furniture breaking. He had collected energy, but not stored it. Across the room his coffee table lay in many burnt pieces, a third of it where the blast had hit was missing completely. Mary Jane woke with a start, "What happened?"

"I wasn't ready," John said. "I was flying through the stars and I panicked. We may be dealing with things more dangerous than I imagined."

"It's okay baby," said Mary Jane giving him a kiss. "We just have to practice more."

Next on the list was Axton. Their destination was wherever it is you go after death, which meant neither of them had a clue as to how they should proceed. "We just have to connect to the other side, right?" asked Mary Jane.

"I don't know. Is there only one other side or could there be many? I am sure it will happen when we need it to. Maybe we should keep looking for more people."

"That might be a good idea. We have made a lot of progress already talking to others like us. It is getting late. I think we should rest first."

They were both lying on opposite sides of John's queen bed. John had his hands folded, and in any other location he might be mistaken for a dead man. He was controlling his breathing and entering a meditative state. He was missing the obvious chance to get closer to the beautiful new girl in his life. On some level, there was no him, there was no her, and there was no bed. He was too distracted with his no-mind state that came from connecting to the other side. Mary Jane leaned over and kissed him on the cheek. "Thank you for coming for me John," she said, before preparing herself to connect with the other side as she drifted into sleep.

Chapter 9
The Man With No Face

It couldn't have been very far into the night when John started to hear the soothing sound of the ocean. He opened his eyes to find himself once again on the beach. Howard, who was standing over him started to speak, "Don't worry, John, you are not fully here. The meditative dream state allows us both to communicate without crossing over fully. There is something I have to tell you. It's a story. My story. Listen very closely. You may have guessed this, but you were not my first pupil. There were many others before you." The scene changed to what you would get if you crossed a dojo with a temple. A few rows of students appeared, sitting before their master, Howard, who was at the front of the room in a Zen like state. "The man who is after you," continued Howard, "used to be one of my students."

John walked through the memory like a ghost, observing the students, and the classroom. He noticed that one of them, even at a young age, was wearing the same mask he had observed on the man at the coffee shop. As Howard continued, the masked student's eyes seemed to follow John even though there was no possible way of him knowing John would one day witness this memory. "He was the most advanced of any students I have ever had." Other scenes came flooding into John's vision, all of the masked pupil demonstrating advanced knowledge. John had never witnessed anything like this. He knew that most of the things he was witnessing were going to be part of his training as well. Instead of carrying heavy objects like the rest of the students, the masked student allowed them to levitate with little difficulty. "I thought he was destined to be the next great leader, but he was always hungry for more. It was like the whole world was a bore to him. Soon he started ignoring the other pupils and taking control of everything he could." John saw more scenes that defied the laws of physics. The masked student started fires with his mind, created material objects out of nothing and easily surpassed all others doing the postures they were given.

"One day, the other students joined together to rebel against him," Howard continued. "They would not have such a tyrannical ruler, and even my own ability to protect them was blinded by my greed for such an advanced student to take over my role. They had found a spell, one with ancient words of great power.

One of the ancient words you have already been introduced to, Apertambuxtion, but these students were not ready for such a powerful force. They did not know what they were doing or what would happen when they tried to banish him. They bound him hand and foot while he was sleeping, and carried him outside to the circle they had made in the dirt. With four posts of fire facing in each direction, they started to carry out their intentions through this ancient incantation. At the time I was meditating nearby and came as quickly as I could, when I heard the commotion. Even the other teachers were there with the students, including my own brother. I can still feel the shame of seeing him as part of the crowd, taking out his frustration on my star pupil. Filled with rage I tried to stop them, but my brother knew everything I would try to do to stop them, and he held me back. Then, as they were finishing the final part of their tyranny, everything stopped.

Time froze completely around me, and my star pupil released his bonds, walking over to me calmly."

John witnessed the scene, a small mob of angry people surrounding the masked student. He saw the look of pain in Howard's face at this moment, his most dear possession about to be taken away from him. Frozen in time, the masked student walked over to Howard who was on his knees being held up by both arms, and started to speak.

"Do not cry for what has been done or what we are to become. There is still one yet you must teach." Handing a slip of paper to Howard, the masked student continued, "You will need this. It will be his first lesson. The man who frees you from your prison."

As tears fell from Howard's eyes, he looked up at the masked student who was beyond any of this and spoke, "I'm sorry. I am so sorry. I should have seen it sooner. I neglected everyone else for you. Forgive me."

The masked student brought his face much closer to Howard and spoke, "He will come to you one day, and you must teach him. He will truly become your best student. Then we will both be forgiven."

When his sentence ended time resumed back to normal, but there was a change. Howard was now in the middle of the circle. With a look of shock on everybody's face, it was too late to stop. There was a scream from Howard that seemed to be pulled out of the very fabric of the universe as his body disappeared completely and the masked student was left standing there. Everybody in the crowd took a step back in fright, knowing what was coming next. The man in the mask once again seemed to be staring through Howard's memory and looking straight into John's eyes. There was an all out panic as people tried to run away shouting and screaming and falling to the side as they tried to attack the Masked Man. But Howard's memory of what happened next was blank, as he was no longer there.

The scene turned blank, then back to the beach. John saw a faded version of the younger Howard laying on the beach, having appeared there with a scream and tears in his eyes. He struck his fist in the sand and his head was hanging low. "And that is how I got here," said Howard. "Cast out unwittingly by my own family. I am still ashamed of what happened, as I imagine they are. I am so sorry, John. I had to tell you because I need you to know that none of us are perfect. You will face many difficult trials on your journey. I was sent here for a reason, by my own disgrace. Please know that there will be times you make the wrong choice. I pray it does not cost you the time and pain that it has cost me. You were the first person to appear here since I was banished. I am led to believe the Masked Man knew all of this would happen, and that it would be you who was led here. I don't know what he wants of you John, but right now he is one step ahead. Watch out for him and do not confront him. His power is much greater than yours or mine. Our time is up. Remember to be vigilant and always aware of your surroundings. Respond with understanding, instead of thoughtlessly reacting."

The beach, along with Howard, and the sounds of the ocean, faded. John was brought back to his bed, to the sound of his own beating heart. With tears rolling down his face and Mary Jane now cuddling up next to him, John lay motionless in his bed with more questions than ever.

Over breakfast John told Mary Jane the story of what he had seen the night before. "I still can't get it out of my head, the way he looked at me. He was staring right at me, like he knew I was there, even though it was just a memory," John said to her.

Mary Jane tried to make him feel better with her words: "It was just a coincidence. No one could be *that* powerful and all-knowing. You are not alone in this, I am here for you. If you ever need to talk or open up to someone, remember that I am here."

"Thank you. I know all of this is completely insane and... and I don't even know how to deal with it myself. It is all so new and foreign. I don't know how much of it I even believe. What if we really are crazy? I don't want to end up like my mother. What if we should have listened to the Masked Man in the coffee shop, and gone back to our normal lives instead of putting all of this pressure on us to be superheroes," John said, starting to question himself.

Mary Jane looked like she was about to smack him as she said, "Don't talk like that, John. You know how uncomfortable it was to be a part of that lie. Neither of us ever fit in, or felt like things were right, and now we finally know why. I wouldn't give that up for anything. We found each other. We were meant to find each other and we always will. Now we have the rest of our lives together. I know there will be unpleasant things we have to go through before we can focus our attention on each other, but I'm not worried about it. Nothing would be worth losing this freedom, look how far you have gotten already. You know as well as I do that this was a chance at something better. A chance to live a real life instead of one in prison."

John looked at her with sad eyes. Even before she said any of it he had felt the same way. It was a moment of weakness when he turned a slight desperation into something he didn't even want to say. Had Mary Jane wanted him to say it? It was part of John's path, and an outside observer may never know whether it was John who said it or something beyond. It had to be said because it *was* said. With new-found resolve and strength, John sat up straight, and pulled himself together, looking ten times more macho.

"You're right," he said. "We will get through this together. If there is anyone at all I would want to go through this with, it is you. Something has been bringing us together from the very start, and I am going to do everything I can to make it work."

John got up from his chair and put his arms around Mary Jane as he was speaking. She had completely changed his world, as he had hers. There was no turning back now.

Chapter 10
The Plan

After an uneventful day of meditation and restlessness, John and Mary Jane went to bed. Mary Jane seemed to move through the postures and lessons with ease, getting along from one pose to the next with little effort, while John was watching with embarrassment, pretending not to be out of breath. That night, John had a different sort of dream. If it even was a dream. He was walking through a courtyard, toward a building. All along the path, there were bronze statues of children, in all different poses. Playing, laughing, walking, and interacting with each other. All of them lifeless children, frozen in time. It was as if he were moving through a playground that had paused, as John approached the building. He was walking toward the front of this house and saw something out of the corner of his eye. John spun around and saw one of the statues casting a creepy stare in his direction. John approached the statue, caught by its gaze. As he got closer the eyes of the statue became more and more real. When he was standing right in front of it, the eyes were completely lifelike and following his every move. The statue struggled to speak through it's tight bronze lips, "Help me." As soon as he heard the words John's attention turned to the Masked Man who had come out of the house.

"What are you going to do, John?" asked the Masked Man. "Standing there all alone waiting for someone to save him... ha ha ha ha... you disappoint me. You're not even going to ask him why he is here, are you?"

John woke with a start. The dream was fading away while he laid in bed, with his eyes now open, trying to remember and hold on to every last detail. "I found Axton," were the first words to escape from John's mouth, "The Cleaner said he was dead. How can we tell him his son suffers a fate worse than death? We have to rescue him... but how? We have to keep learning. There has to be something in the book about living statues, right?" John finished his statement as a question.

"How can we expect to do anything while the Masked Man is there?" Mary Jane asked. She knew his dream even though he had not spoken of it.

"I think he lives there. It looked like some sort of training facility as well as Chateau."

"Well, leave it to a super villain to have good taste," said Mary Jane jokingly. "It's lucky for him no one else knows who he is or can see the people trapped as living statues."

"There is something else I just remembered. Before I woke up, the man in the mask did bring up something interesting. He asked me if I was going to ask Axton why he was there."

"You mean, what if he is better off there? Do you think he did something... I mean, he must have done something the Masked Man didn't like, right?"

"Anyone who is against the Masked Man is on our side, so my vote is to save him, but I don't think we are ready for a full on assault. The Masked Man could be there waiting for us."

"What if I distract him?" asked Mary Jane.

"How would you do that? He could kill you. Do you think it's possible?" All that and more questions spilled out of John in one big burst.

"I'll tell him that I can help him find you. I am positive he will give me a chance to betray you."

"No. He'll see right through it. What would make you leave me for no reason?"

"I'll tell him that I am impressed with his power. No one can resist self-flattery. He will have to listen to me if I fawn over him, and tell him how great he is compared to you," Mary Jane replied.

John didn't look very happy as he said, "Fine. I don't like it, but we have to save Axton, and this may be the only way. I want you to know that you don't have to do this. It is a huge risk we would be taking."

"It is my choice. If we save him it will be worth it, but how do we get there if we don't know where it is?"

"I was there last night while I was sleeping. That means I have had a connection with the space and should be able to open the same gateway. I know you don't like traveling this way, but I think I will have to zap us there," John answered.

"I **don't** like traveling that way," said Mary Jane. "But can you at least use a less dangerous sounding word than zap?"

"Deal." They both started doing the postures and getting ready for the meditation. "I haven't taken anyone else with me before. We are both going to have to focus on this to allow it to happen," John said before entering into a meditative state. All that could be heard was the soft sound of their breath in an otherwise silent room. Before they could do any special relocation, the book came back once again, this time to both of them. "Section 3, Material," were the words that appeared before them, floating in the room like superimposed characters of the opening credits of a movie. John wondered what they would look like from different angles. Were the letters really three dimensional? He knew they were just a projection from his own head, but he had also done work with 3D modeling, and these were questions that would bug him any time he saw the section titles floating there.

As the words for the section flowed into their minds they heard a voice reading them aloud: "Section 3, Material. As you know, the entire visible world, which was created to limit, is made of materials. The main material is energy, which was used in many different forms." John noticed that this section seemed more informative and informational like a standard textbook that they give you in public school. A lot of information at once, luckily it was inside of their minds and required no memorization.

"As you may have noticed, materials are all different types and sizes." A window opened in the middle of the room to what looked like an old timey film reel that was showing different objects as the text continued. "You'll find hard ones (a picture of a man using a hammer was shown), soft ones (feathers floated down the screen), wet ones (a picture of a man pouring milk appeared), sharp ones (a knife was shown stuck into a table), and many more (the window was divided into nine sections all showing different scenes of people with objects). What most people don't know, is that our minds have complete control over the very atoms these materials are made of. Energy can be manipulated at will. With experience, you will be able to manipulate any material or object just by thinking about it. You can also change the material of objects at will. This can be as monumental as turning a national treasure into jelly, or as simple as changing the color of your hair. Here are the lessons you will need to start adapting materials at will."

John and Mary Jane both looked up slightly as their heads were filled with the instructions for adapting and creating materials. "Ha, what a rush," John said.

"And just in time too," started Mary Jane. "We will need this to change Axton back into flesh."

"I wonder if all statues used to be people?"

"Obviously, most of them used models for their carving."

John smiled knowing she was being sarcastic and noticing his own mistake. "Are you ready?"

"As ready as I will ever be," she replied.

They did the previous postures, along with a few new ones the book had given them for this section, then sat down to meditate. John concentrated his full awareness on the Chateau, while Mary Jane focused on opening herself to travel with John along the same path. It was about half an hour later that a doorway opened up in the middle of the room. John's concentration had allowed for a physical manifestation of a gateway instead of just taking them directly. They both walked through the door, where they could see statues of children playing leading up to the Chateau.

Chapter 11
The Chateau

"I better go first," said Mary Jane. "I will walk up the path and distract the Masked Man while you save Axton. He must have sensed the dimensional opening by now, so we have to act quickly."

"All right… and, Mary Jane?"

"Yes?"

"I love you," he replied. She looked at him for a second in surprise, then kissed him hard before speed walking up the pathway, past the statues, toward the main entrance of the beautiful building that was fit for a king.

Most of the way to the house she wondered why she was running and slowed down a bit to catch her breath. The air seemed different here. As she approached the massive doors, the one on the right opened for her. She paused for a moment of thought, and then gathered the strength to step into the lion's den. The door had been opened by the Futuristic Man, who had been startled by her presence in the coffee shop. This time he was calm and collected, and he had much fancier clothing.

"Welcome," he said, "the Master is expecting you." As he was speaking, a dozen people came out and kneeled on either side of the pathway that lead into the main hall. Mary Jane wondered if they were bowing for her or for the Master. "Both, respectively," said the Futuristic Man. "You see, we have been waiting a long time to finally meet you. Things are going splendidly."

"Don't you wonder why I am here?" asked Mary Jane.

"Oh heaven's no," replied the Futuristic Man. "The Master knows everything. It is none of my concern why you are here, we are just so happy to see you. You and John are among the most respected of our converts, though you don't know it yet. He he he. My dear only what was meant to happen can happen. Why should we fear the good, the bad, or even the possibility of anything else? We live in the moment and enjoy every bit of it. The Master has created a paradise on earth for us here."

"What kind of paradise freezes people into statues?" asked Mary Jane.

"What makes you think they didn't deserve it?" asked the Futuristic Man. "You are both still naive I see. Why can't you understand that only what has been destined can happen? Only what was meant to be, ever will be. It is impossible for otherwise. But we must not waste time with trifles, come with me to meet the Master." Mary Jane nodded and followed the pathway that seemed to gather with more and more people who were kneeling on either side. She noticed they were all smiling, when they took a moment to stop averting their gaze and sneak a glimpse of her. If anything, this was a much warmer welcome than she expected. As she entered the main hall she could only think of medieval days when the king sat on a massive throne with all of his people gathered around the court. The Masked Man was indeed sitting on a throne. Mary Jane pondered for a moment, thinking that this was the first time she had seen an actual throne, besides in the bathroom. The Masked Man, or Master, if you will, stood up and took a bow. The main room was filling with more and more people who were gathering around to witness this historic occasion. The Master started to speak, "Ahhh, welcome Mary Jane. It is an extreme pleasure to have you here. I hope Jimmy has been treating you well." The Master motioned toward the Futuristic Man who nodded.

So that's his name, thought Mary Jane, just in case she ever had a formal occasion to introduce him to someone else. Sir Reginald, this is Jimmy, the Futuristic Man, Jimmy the Futuristic Man, this is Sir Reginald. A distinct pleasure I assure you, now watch out for his balls of lightening, they could leave you in a pile of ashes.

"My dear you are so lovely. It is a pleasure to have you standing here before me, starting everything. I just love watching it all play out. It almost brings tears to my eyes. The universe simply knows the best way to do everything doesn't it?" said the Master.

Mary Jane had lost some of her confidence at this point, as it seemed she had no control over the situation. Things were either going much better, or much worse than she imagined.

"I want to join you," said Mary Jane. "I'm tired of hanging around the weak."

"Ha ha ha," the Master laughed. "Do you think I'm a fool? I know you're not here to join me, but what you don't know is that you really are here to join me. We will come to that later though. I know you don't want me to know it but your darling John is out there in my courtyard about to free one of the most dangerous criminals known to mankind. Why didn't you listen to me and ask him who he was before you set him free?"

Mary Jane's mouth fell open, something she didn't think actually happened when people were in shock, but just in dramatic movies. There was a tingling feeling of forced awareness that made itself present in the back of her head, encompassing it entirely. She turned around and started to run toward the entrance, but the great doors of the main hall closed as she approached them and swarms of people quickly blocked the way. "My dear," started the Master. "You can't save him now."

As soon as he saw Mary Jane walk into the Chateau, John started sneaking his way along the path as if anybody could be watching. After about thirty seconds he noticed there were other people around him, but they were paying him no mind. They were doing all sorts of things, sitting around a fountain talking, meditating, and even doing the same postures John had been doing not so long ago. That is when John decided it would be safer to walk normally, as he had been fitting in anyway. He approached the bronze statue of Axton, and heard the cry once more, "Help me." The lips were not moving.

"Don't worry buddy, I'll have you out of there in no time," John said. Then John closed his eyes and put his hand on the statue. He focused on flesh, and making this into a living person. The bronze started to melt away, slowly converting into soft flesh. As the bronze on Axton's face started to wear away John noticed that he had suffered severe burns.

John heard the Master's voice in his head, "Now there is someone who should be wearing a mask, huh John? Ha ha ha." The statue of Axton, now half man reached out and grabbed John's arm with his still bronze hand. John's arm started to turn into bronze, which he will attest, was the most painful thing that had ever happened to him. As Axton's hand turned back into skin and bones, John's arm did so as well. Axton let out a huge gasp, it had been a long time since he took a real breath, then collapsed on the ground.

Out of breath, Axton tried to show his gratitude, "Oh, thank you. Thank you so much. It was horrible in there. Agh. We have to get out of here."

"Are you all right?" asked John. "Your Dad sent us to find you."

"Oh thank God," said Axton. "I thought I would be there forever. We have to get to my Dad. Take us out of here."

If John had been paying more attention, he would have noticed the two of them were now encircled by all of the people who had been standing around the courtyard. They stood passively not making a move, but John knew if he tried anything they would grab him. "Do it," said Axton. "Do it now." Before John had time to consider that they were approaching because of Axton, and not because of him, John focused his mind on taking them out of there. With Axton's desperate cries in the otherwise silence of a blissful Chateau courtyard, the only sound that came next was one you've probably never heard before. It was the sound of the other side ripping open and pulling them through to John's apartment. Axton was now on the floor weeping with the overwhelming joy of getting out of his prison. John was standing over him with his eyes closed and hands held out.

Chapter 12

Getting off Track

"Get my Dad," Axton said through his tears, still heaving and coughing, learning to breath once again.

"I will. You just rest for now. Take a shower and I'll make coffee," said John. Axton was elated, and that is no exaggeration. It was really something to be back in the real world, a living person able to interact, and do everything things we take for granted. Something as simple as swiping a bird away from your shoulder. Axton nodded. John showed him where the towels were, and how to turn on the water, then got a pair of clothes ready for him. They were not quite the same size, but John had a few articles of clothing that were too big for him, and looked like they would fit Axton. It wasn't that the clothes Axton was wearing were out of date so much as they were tattered and pretty much wrecked. They revealed as much as they covered. It must have been part of the unfreezing process. The clothes must have been burned and deteriorated from the bronze and back conversion.

Axton started to shower while John went to the kitchen and started making coffee. He got filtered water from the refrigerator while the beans were grinding in his automatic coffee grinder, then put them in the coffee maker as one typically does when making coffee. John knew that the secrets to good coffee were the beans, the grind, cold filtered water, and the perfect brewing temperature to allow all of the oils of the bean to flavor every drop. If Axton had been in better shape, and this had been a normal day, John would have taken time to explain every step of the process to Axton. As far as John knew, only he and the coffee shop down the street had anything close to perfect coffee, but it also took a good state of mind. A meditative state. You have to do everything with love and attention if you want it to come out perfectly. There is just that extra touch that makes it incredible instead of very good, but I digress.

As the coffee was brewing John picked up the Grime Fighter's card that was on his kitchen table. He dialed the number and heard it ringing. "Grime Fighter's, are you calling to report a grime?" came the voice on the other end of the line. It was Jeff, the head Grime Fighter, owner of Grime Fighters. John didn't know it but Jeff was still salty about a rival company, Partners in Grime, who had asked him about his business before starting their own with a similar name.

John stifled a laugh at the cheesy line Jeff had used upon answering the phone, then became more serious. "I found Axton," said John, not wanting to beat around the bush with someone who had been put through so much already.

"You did? Oh thank God, where is he? Is he okay? Is he safe?" asked Jeff.

"Yes, he is here with me right now taking a shower," answered John. There was silence on the line.

"Wait, he is there with you? I told you to find him, not bring him back here," said Jeff loudly, with an air of concern. "Listen to me, don't do anything until I get there. I'm coming right now and will be there as fast as I can. I'm literally two minutes away." The line clicked as Jeff hung up abruptly. Jeff didn't seem to be as happy as John thought he would be to hear that his son was back.

John sat at the table tensely, drinking his coffee. The phone call left a bad taste in his mouth, a taste that was quickly washed away by amazing coffee. Axton finished showering and got dressed. He walked into the kitchen and poured himself a cup of coffee. "So, what's the word?" Axton asked John.

"Your Dad is coming. He didn't sound as enthusiastic as I thought he would about you being here," John answered.

"Relax, it's hard to see someone after being away from them for so long. I mean, he thought he lost me, and that we would never see each other again. You've proven him wrong, John. I thank you for that. Things are going to be different from now on. I can finally have the life I want." John nearly dropped his coffee when the front door swung open as Jeff, The Cleaner, burst through.

"Get away from him," said Jeff. John was not sure if he was talking to him or to Axton, but clearly he wanted them separated. Jeff continued over to the table and it became clear he was angry with Axton. "Why did you bring him back here?" he demanded, giving John an angry look. "He was better off where he was."

"Awww, it's good to see you too, Dad," said Axton. "Do you have any idea how long I've been waiting for this? I so badly need energy, and you have always been able to channel it so well. I just need a little to get started, I've been frozen for so long, and had nothing to charge on."

"You should have never found out about that book. John, we have to send him back, he is hungry for power, and he will never be satisfied until he has taken all of it from innocent people," Jeff said, trying to illicit help from John.

"There is an easier way," said Axton. "Why don't you teach me to connect the way you do so I can get the power directly. Then no one has to get hurt."

"It doesn't belong to you, it belongs to the entire universe. John, grab his arms and help me," said Jeff.

John was caught between two people having a family argument, or so he thought. He didn't know what they were fighting about, or who to believe. Axton seemed like a normal person, and John was still sympathetic because Axton had been stuck as a statue for who knows how long. Jeff approached Axton with force, but Axton stood up and grabbed Jeff before he had a chance to do anything.

"I guess I'll have to settle for what you do have," said Axton. Jeff started to turn white and it was noticeable that Axton was draining his energy. I am sure Jeff would have been screaming if the air hadn't been sucked out of his lungs during the process. He let out something like an inhalation gasp that ended with a pop and a pile of clothes and ash where Jeff had been standing not long ago.

"Oh relax," said Axton to John. "You saw what he was going to do."

"But… he was your father," said John in a small voice. He was in a state of awe at the sight he had just witnessed. "Are you going to do that to anybody else?"

"No, of course not. Not yet. John, I still need you buddy! You've got to help me find the book!" said Axton with a grin. Axton took a sip of coffee still grinning wide. "Man, this coffee is amazing! You sure know how to brew it." The scars and burn marks on his face healed with a white glow that seemed to be under his skin. He stretched out his face muscles and spoke, "Agh. That feels soooo much better. How do I look? I was worried I would have to wear a mask the rest of my life. That should be something you choose to do, not something that is forced on you because other people can't stand their own shame when they look at you."

'What have I gotten myself into?' is all that John could think at that moment, 'At least Mary Jane is safe.'

"Are you up for another space jump?" Axton asked John. "We need to get to the Temple. That's the last place I had the book."

"What is to stop me from going alone and leaving you here?"

"Aww, now that would hurt my feelings, John. After all we've been through together, I would hate to have to kill you over something so stupid. I know how to follow you through the gateway, buddy, I just can't open it myself right now. Maybe if I had all of your power I could, would you prefer I try that?" Axton said to him. John felt a wave of discomfort go through him at the idea of being sucked into dust. For now he would have to play along.

Mary Jane was watching all of this on a window the Master had created, floating in mid-air. This one was two dimensional on most of it's sides, but on the one Mary Jane was facing, she could watch what John was doing.

"Do you think you can save him?" the Master asked Mary Jane. "I can't. The bronze statue thing only works once. The only way to stop that lunatic now is to kill him. Would you do that to save your darling John?"

"There has to be another way," said Mary Jane, she did not want to consider killing someone even if it was for the love of her life.

"You really haven't known him that long, couldn't you just let him go, and find someone else?" asked the Master.

"You don't understand, we are meant to be together. We have been drawn together and it is meant to be. Nothing else can be!"

The Master sighed and shook his head. "I understand perfectly well. You know what? I do have someone else who would be willing to kill him, but let's just watch John suffer some more first, shall we?"

"You monster," Mary Jane shouted at him. "Let me out of here!"

"Say, now there's an idea," the Master said out loud, not quite talking to Mary Jane so much as himself. "I'll tell you what, take this and you can save him," he said to her. Mary Jane felt her hand get heavier because of something she was now holding. It was a gun. "How much do you really love him?" the Master asked her. Mary Jane didn't hesitate, she pointed the gun at the Master and pulled the trigger. CLICK. It didn't fire. The Master started laughing, "Ha, you really hate me that much don't you? You would let John die where he is, just so you could kill me right now."

"I would have found a way to save him," said Mary Jane. The gun disappeared.

Chapter 13
The Temple of Gloom

By this point John had already taken Axton to the Temple. John still wasn't sure where the Temple was, but he had been there in Howard's memory. That allowed him to visualize the area and bring them there. The Temple was falling apart; in all likelihood, no one had been there in years, and what was left, was totally burned.

"They must have abandoned it after I burned them for trying to send me away," said Axton, "If you ask me, they are the real monsters. All I ever wanted to do was learn." They searched through the various buildings uncovering all kinds of things that had been left behind in a hurry. "I can't find it," said Axton. "It's strange, I can feel the book's presence, but I can't figure out where it is. It must have left energy behind when it was taken from here."

"Why is this book so important?" asked John.

"It tells you everything. It *is* everything. The book is the way, it is the gateway. It gives you all the knowledge for everything in the universe, and they took that away from me!" Then it finally clicked. Axton was looking for the book that was in John's head. He was lucky they were by the Temple when Axton noticed the energy from it, or Axton might already know where the book was. If John could keep him searching, maybe he could figure out a plan in the meantime.

"Where did you get it in the first place?"

Axton replied, "It was given to me by my teacher. I worked so hard to get where I was, and he rewarded me by giving me the book. Things were coming along nicely. I had learned to tap into energy sources, as you saw back at the house. Then one day I was woken up in the middle of the night, and dragged out of my room, like some kind of animal. Then there was the fire... I shouldn't be talking about this. If the book is not here we need to find out where it is, and I know the next place we need to look. I have been there before. When I was young, my dad took me there. It's called The Library. It is a place beyond this world, which is why I need your help to get there. I can open the memory, and you can connect with it, then you'll take us through the doorway."

"Can we go somewhere more comfortable? This place is a little... burnt."

"Aww, don't say that. This used to be a very comfortable space. Haven't you learned to manipulate time yet? This space is beyond perfect for what we need to do. There used to be so much energy here." Alex had a glazed look of nostalgia on his face that would have been warm to anyone who wasn't thinking of him sucking the life out of people.

"Manipulate time? No, I haven't learned that, is it even possible?"

"Pssshh. Is it even possible? HA! You have a long way to go, little man. It was one of the first things the book taught me," said Axton, "But we don't have the book yet, now do we?"

John understood that the book appeared in different ways to different people. It all depended on where they were on their path, and where they needed to go. If you got the wrong lesson at the wrong time, it would kill you... or someone else... maybe you would end up with a tuba for a left arm and two legs made of giant strawberries. That might be getting off lightly, but it would still make walking very difficult in neighborhoods with fruit loving dogs.

Everything would be unpredictable if the book weren't part of the balance and connection of the universe. Since the book was connected, only what was meant to happen would ever be possible. Could the book ever be another way? Of course not... because it wasn't. Only that which was meant to happen could ever happen. Then why was he still afraid? His mind was still grasping for control. "If you read it in the book, then you can do it, right?" John asked.

"Hmmm... Let me see," said Axton. He stood still with his eyes closed for a minute, then opened them wide and said, "Yes! There is enough residual energy left in this space from what happened. I can probably absorb it, and use it to restore at least the main Temple so we can concentrate." Axton lifted his arms and John, being connected with the other side, could see the energy being pulled from all around, and absorbed into Axton. The space was suddenly colder, and felt like a graveyard. It was all still and silent. Axton said a few words that John didn't understand: "Ashta siddhi nav nidhi ke dhata, asabara dina janaki mata," and the building that John assumed was the main Temple (because it started glowing), slowly changed from a broken down building into a peaceful Temple that was warm and comfortable (which John found out when he entered). "It's not perfect, but it should last long enough for us to get to The Library. Concentrate on my thoughts, John, and then take us out of here."

They were both inside the Temple at this point, sitting on comfortable zafu. Upon sitting cross-legged, John's mind wandered to what the plural for zafu was. Was it zafu's? Zafusses? Zafi?

"Concentrate!" Axton scolded him, "I can feel your thoughts wandering. The mind does that on purpose to hold you back. It is afraid of losing control, and this is way past the point of no return. Let go of everything it says, and you will be able to take us to The Library."

"Sorry," said John. He sat still and let go of his thoughts. When everything seemed empty and calm, he heard Axton telling him to get up. They were at The Library.

"Don't trust him, John!" Mary Jane yelled at the floating window. Though there was still a long way to go in her education, it was noticeable to her that time was different at the Chateau. It felt like she had been standing there for only a few minutes, even though John had been through hours of adventure. Adventure. Mary Jane thought about the word. It was the wrong word for the situation. Adventure usually implies enjoyment, or at least consent. John was being held hostage by a psychopath that might turn him into dust without notice. Not that notice would make it better, in fact the opposite. Then he would have to stand there waiting for it to happen. Was it painful or just a puff of smoke? It was beside the point, but you can see why Mary Jane and John were good for each other, if not for their dissociative feelings, but for the way their minds worked. "You have to get him away from that lunatic," she shouted to the Master, clearly more upset than John was about the situation.

"I don't," said the Master. "But like I said, I have someone who will." The Master snapped his fingers and out walked a beautiful girl with green hair. It was Mary Jane. Was it a copy of her? No, it was too perfect. This person was her, but at a different point in time. Did she really change sides and start working for the Master? How could she betray John like that? Maybe she remembered this exact situation, and knew she had to stay with the Master and cooperate so she would be given this opportunity to go back to save John. The Master looked at the new Mary Jane and said to her, "Go and take care of this. Make sure he doesn't suspect anything about you. He needs to be on our side, and you are the best way to make that happen. Make sure he loves you. Take him out to dinner, go on dates, everything normal people do so that he trusts you."

"He'll know it isn't me!" said Mary Jane, fighting her own conclusion that this girl was her.

"Ha," the Master laughed. "It is you! Time doesn't work the way people think it does. You are going to be here with me for a lifetime my dear, and this is when you finally get to leave, right now, to go and save your precious John at The Library. Of course, I could let him die instead if you prefer."

Mary Jane hated the idea of John being hurt, even if it meant he had to spend the rest of his life with... wait a minute, should she feel bad about this if it really was her? She should know what to do now in order to get back to this point again: gain the trust of the Master so he would send her back to save John. If it was still her then John was always the priority. How long would she have to stay with the Master? "A long time," said the other Mary Jane. "It will take a long time, but there is so much you don't know yet. The Master is the answer. He will teach you everything. I know right now the book seems like the most important thing, but he will show you so much more. He is the most powerful and connected with the other side. He will save us all. He will bring about freedom to all who choose this path. Just look at the paradise he has created here. Now if memory serves me, this is where I leave." The other Mary

Jane disappeared with a flash, and was now visible on the window that was showing The Library.

"This is where you stop watching," said the Master. "We can't have you knowing too much about your own future. It will all make sense in time." Mary Jane was furious that he closed the window. She would not know what happened next... until it was her going there to save John.

"Why are you doing this?" she shouted at the Master.

"Let me show you why," he replied to her. The Master walked up to her, only a few feet away, and took off his mask. Mary Jane's face lost all color. Her hair started turning green as she fell onto her back, trying to pull herself away toward the door. What happened from there comes later, we have to go back to John now.

Chapter 14

Here & Now

John and Axton were in a small hallway with a plain white-collar office type door at the end. There was a sign on the door that read, "The Library." To be honest John was disappointed. "Are you sure this is it?" he said to Axton.

"This is just the entrance. It's like that so it doesn't draw attention." As if people would stumble upon it by accident, John thought to himself. Axton opened the door and gave John the invitation to enter with the swing of his hand. John took a step in, and couldn't believe it. The Library was shelves upon shelves of books with no end in sight.

"It must be the size of a small country," said John.

They were greeted by the voice of an older man with a long white beard. "Ah, yes it is. It might even be as big as a large country. The Library contains a copy of every book ever written, whether the original still exists or not. It's a godsend in some ways, but you wouldn't believe how many unfinished novels there are from people who fancied themselves writers. Heh heh. I'm sorry, I didn't introduce myself. I am The Librarian. People used to call me James, back before I got stuck here, but since then I have only been known as The Librarian. I doubt anybody living would even remember me anyway. You see, time is different in The Library."

He was interrupted by Axton, "Yes, we know about how time works here. We need you to help us find a book."

"Oh. Did you also know that there has to be one person here all the time? I didn't. That is how they tricked me into staying here all these years. I've enjoyed it though... and read almost all of them. They do keep appearing you know? Very curious, indeed, it is, and yes, of course I can help you find a book. If there is anyone who can, it is me. Maybe we can help each other. Ahhh... it's you. I remember you. You used to come here with your dad when you were little. What ever happened to him anyway, a real nice man he was. Jeffery, it was that they called him, if memory serves me." said The Librarian.

"He has moved on," said Axton, shaking his head with an almost believable air of solace.

"I'm sorry to hear that. A great man he was, as I said."

"I'm afraid we don't have a lot of time," said Axton impatiently, "We need your help finding a book. The book. It doesn't have a title." John knew the title but was in no rush to help Axton to acquire the book. You may have a brief moment of awe if you remember it yourself, if not, look at the cover of this book.

"Well, I don't know if I can help you find anything without a title," said The Librarian, "everything here has a name."

"You know exactly which book I mean," said Axton coldly. "It's the one my father said to stay away from. He wouldn't even show me where it was. He just told me if I ever felt anything to stay away."

"Ahh," said The Librarian, his smile fading, "I do know which book you mean. But you should listen to your father. Stay away from it. If you are meant to read it, the book will come to you."

They walked slowly through the halls of The Library (The Librarian was not as young as he used to be, and Axton would have happily gone on without him, if only they knew where he was taking them). Eventually, they came to a side room that was locked. "This is the private collection," The Librarian told them, as if anyone could even find The Library in the first place, yet alone reach some secret section of it. The door opened to reveal a large room with a pedestal. On it was a beam of light shining on a holder, where there should have been a book. There was someone in the room with their back turned. Someone with green hair.

"Give me the book," said Axton threateningly, noticing that she was holding it. She turned around and the book vanished. Axton lost it. "Get it back! Give it to me," he shouted at her.

Mary Jane held up her hand, and a glowing golden ball appeared floating a few inches above her palm. "You know what this is, don't you?" she said to Axton. John had no idea what was going on at this point or how Mary Jane was there, but he was very glad to see her. If the situation was not so dangerous, he would have paid more attention to her hair, which was now a beautiful forest green as it had been the first time he saw her.

"I do," said Axton. "You are going to turn me into bronze?" he asked her cautiously.

"Stay right where you are. We are going to leave this place, and you are going to be the new Librarian," said Mary Jane. How did she know so much? Where did the orb come from? All kinds of questions needed answering for John, but the more pressing matter was getting out of there, and away from the lunatic who was turning people to ash.

They locked the door to the private room with Axton still inside. They could hear his voice through the door saying, "You made the wrong move." The amount of time it took them to get back to the entrance was more than it should have been because the current Librarian was having a hard time keeping up. John wanted to sit down, and meditate them all out of there, but The Librarian told them they could only do that after they left the main entrance. By the time they got to the exit, Axton was already there waiting for them. He grabbed Mary Jane by the arm. "I can't let you leave me here. Go ahead and turn me back into bronze if you want. Something tells me that you can't or you would have already," said Axton, calling her bluff. Mary Jane was clearly in pain, Axton was starting to steal her energy.

"Let go of her," John yelled, pushing Axton away.

"Oh no, I'm not letting any of you go. You had your chance to make this easy, now you are going to give me back my book or all of you are going to die here," Axton said, taking a step closer.

"Get your hand off of her!" a voice said from behind them. It was Jeff, Axton's father who had been turned to dust so recently.

"What? How are you here?" Axton asked, feeling less confident.

"You think you're so tough. You've always been weak. That's why you had to steal power from everyone else. Let them go, and come over here right now," Jeff said. Axton walked over to him and reached his arm out to grab Jeff, but his hand went right through. It was just a projection of him. "Get out now," Jeff yelled to the others who were already halfway through the door.

"No!" cried out Axton, running over to the entrance. He tried to follow them but an invisible force stopped him from going any further. Axton was now trapped in The Library. He was the new Librarian, and he had all the time in the world to read every book ever written. Except the only thing he wanted to.

The vision of Jeff appeared to the group who so narrowly escaped being consumed. "You're safe for now. I have been so connected with energy in my lifetime that I was able to save my consciousness, but not my body. But it's okay. Axton and I can finally spend time together. I am going to stay here with him."

"Thank you," John said to him.

"It had to be this way," Jeff said to him. "It was the only way." Mary Jane knew that was a polite way of saying, 'now you don't have to kill him.' The image of Jeff faded.

John and Mary Jane concentrated, and brought themselves back to John's house along with The Librarian. "Oh my. I'm finally free. I don't know what I will do. It's a miracle," said The Librarian.

"You know we are going to have to stop calling you The Librarian now and go back to your old name, James," said John.

"I just wish I was younger," said James. "I don't know how much longer I will be able to enjoy being free."

Mary Jane lifted her hand out to him face up and the book appeared. "Here, it will be safe with you."

He nodded. "Thank you for trusting me. I will keep it safe, as I did for so many years," said James as he picked up the book. It disappeared again, but this time it was into James' mind. Mary Jane and John watched as James started to get younger before their very eyes. "It will be my life's work to protect this book," James said. "Now I better get going. Thank you both."

John stared on at him wide-eyed. The Librarian had just transformed into the same Futuristic Man who had tried to kill them in the coffee shop. Mary Jane now knew more about the role he was playing in all of this. "Hey

James," called out Mary Jane. "You're young again. I think it's time you started going by Jimmy."

"Yes, I like that," said Jimmy, as he walked toward the front door.

"Shouldn't we stop him?" John asked Mary Jane.

"No," said Mary Jane. "It's about time I tell you a little more about what happened while I was at the Chateau. It wasn't just for a night, I was there for years."

"No," John said in disbelief. "I am so sorry. I'll kill them both. That monster and his lackey."

"Actually, Jimmy helped me through my time there. He is an innocent part of all of this. I will explain it to you some day. Don't worry about it though, everything is okay now John. It was the only way it could be. I was hoping we could forget about all of this for a while and spend some time together. You know, do normal couple things like go to the movies or dinner."

"Anything you want," said John, hugging her tightly.

~~~

"I don't understand," said Mary Jane through tears, still on the floor of the Chateau.

"It's okay," said the Master, tossing his mask to the side. "I will only need this one more time, and not with you," he continued. "Jimmy will show you to your room. You will find it most accommodating. We do have a lot of space here after all. I am sorry, but you will have to stay here for quite some time. I think we will grow very comfortable together, as you noticed on the future version of you. I am not the bad guy. I know it looks that way now, but it all has a bigger reason behind it. It was all planned from the very beginning." The Master walked out of the main hall and left Mary Jane in the capable hands of his right hand man, Jimmy, the Futuristic Man.

~~~

John held Mary Jane all night, even while they slept. Some part of him was so afraid of losing her again. He liked the idea of doing normal things with her, but knew that he would have to keep progressing through the book as well. Were hero's allowed to take a break? Was he a hero? If the universe allowed it, who was he to complain? Mary Jane had tears in her eyes, finally being reunited with him after all of these years, she could fall asleep next to him, comfortable for the first time in so long.

"John," she said turning to face him. "John... I love you. I wish I said it before, but how could I have known I wouldn't see you again for so long?"

"I love you too, Mary Jane," he said back to her, comforting her, and holding her close to him. "I will never let you go." They fell asleep in each other's arms. It was the best sleep Mary Jane had in a long time.

Chapter 15
Jimmy Comforts Mary Jane

Jimmy was doing his best to comfort a reluctant Mary Jane at the Chateau. He showed her to her room, which was the size of a small house. Space didn't matter here. A broom closet could be a mansion. Time and space only mattered as much as you wanted them to. There was no need to eat, sleep, or go to the bathroom, but you could do any of them as you desired. None of them aged here. It was their idea of paradise. Free from any responsibility or obligation in life, down to the very basic need to breathe. Attachment had become unnecessary. For them it was paradise, but for others it would be their own personal hell, people who still thought everything was real. Mary Jane had not had enough time to decide which category she fell in.

Jimmy was very polite to Mary Jane, who was still a bit fearful of him, because of the earlier events at the coffee shop. He had tried to kill her, it seemed, and actually succeeded in destroying John. It was only out of luck that John managed to travel out of there with the energy from the blast. Jimmy started to talk to her in a more serious tone, "Mary Jane, there is something I have to tell you. I know what happens to John once he enters The Library."

"But how could you know that?" Mary Jane asked. "Do you know how to access that world? Have you read the book?"

"Well, yes to both of those. I did read the book, and I do have access to other parts of time, if I so choose. Believe it or not, you are the one who gave me the book. I could show you right now, but I would rather tell you the whole story. The reason I know, is because I was there. I was already in The Library when they arrived," continued Jimmy.

"Did you hurt him?" she asked Jimmy, still unsure of his alliances.

"No, not at all. I didn't even know who he was at the time," started Jimmy. "I had been in The Library for so long before they ever arrived. John came with someone I had seen before, you saw him as a statue earlier. His name is Axton. You're not going to believe it, but you actually saved me that day. I wanted to thank you for that, but knew it needed some explanation first. I remember it well, they both came into The Library together. Axton asked me to find the book for him. I tried to pretend I didn't know what he was talking about, but he saw right through it."

"Why didn't John recognize you?" Mary Jane said, interrupting him.

"Well, at that time I was a lot older. Hard to imagine, isn't it? I had a long white beard, and even if I looked familiar to John, he would never have guessed that I was also the same person as the young man who tried to kill him at the coffee shop, which is a story for another time of course. I wasn't really trying to kill either of you. Anyway, I was taking the two of them to the private section of The Library to give him the book so he wouldn't kill us, and when we got there someone else was already in the room. A beautiful young girl with green hair. That someone was you. The you that the Master sent back today from the main hall. She had the book, and hid it from Axton, then threatened him with this (Jimmy handed her the gold orb). I knew when you got here that I would have to give it to you. It is from the Master's collection, of course. As he mentioned it doesn't work on a person more than once; but Axton didn't figure that out until we got far enough away from him to escape, and leave him trapped as the new Librarian. You see, one person has to stay in The Library, some kind of spell is on it that will not let the last person leave. I was that person for a long time before we trapped him. I want you to know that John is safe, and what's more, he is safe with you."

"John took us out of The Library and back to his house, which is where you gave me the book. I used it to make myself younger before I left. It's a funny thing really, this many years later I finally realized that we had known each other without really knowing each other. I had to come here to tell you this. First to thank you for saving me from an eternity in The Library, but also because I wanted to do something for you. I wanted you to feel more comfortable here. Please understand that you are among friends. We have your best interests in mind, and we are going to do everything we can to make sure things work out for the best, the only way they ever could. I know it was shocking to see the Master like that earlier today. In a strange way, he wants what is best for us too, but you have to remember that he already knows all of it. How it began, and how it is will end. He may do things that don't make a lot of sense right now. Some of them seem cruel and harsh, but his heart is in the right place. He was destined for the role, and if he does something, there is a good reason for it. You will have to trust me on it, even if you don't trust him yet. Something tells me it won't be as hard as you think."

Mary Jane sat back in awe at what she had just heard. It answered so many questions she had, except the most important one, what happened to John? For one thing, she was glad that he was safe, and finally out of the reach of

Axton. "Well that's it for now," Jimmy said. "You keep that orb some place safe so you can save me at The Library. Try to get some sleep, even though you don't really need it here. It helps the emotional state, and is a nice way to let your brain rest. I will leave you alone now. If you need anything at all, think of me, and I will knock on your door. If it feels more urgent, I will appear here in front of you to help."

"Thank you, Jimmy, for telling me what happened, and being here for me. I haven't decided what to think yet. This is all so strange and new to me... but what hasn't been?"

Jimmy nodded and spoke, "You're not alone here." He walked out of the room. She turned off the lights and went to bed, where she would lie awake for what seemed like a few hours, still shaken from the events of the day and from being in this strange new place.

Chapter 16
Advanced Materialization

In his sleep that night, John was once again taken to Howard, at the beach. "I know you were resting, John, but you don't need sleep here. If you use the techniques Jeff taught you to channel the energy of the universe, you won't need sleep where you were either," said Howard.

"How do you know about what Jeff taught me?" asked John.

"I don't know. When you connect to the other side there is no more need to know or remember. Everything is there, all of existence, and you can call upon it if you let go of what your mind is holding on to and understand that you have access to infinite knowledge. Until you let go, you won't be able to connect with the other side on a regular basis. Some of it will still slip through the cracks, like when you say something that is right even though you are not the one who thought to say it. The universe guides you, and gives you what you need, but when you become one with it, then you will be free to decide what and when you give and receive," Howard said to him.

"There is still a lot I would like to know."

"That's understandable. It will all come in time. The more attached you are to wanting it, the longer it will take to get it. I am going to bring you here at night so we can practice the more advanced steps of your training. You already learned about materials, and how to adapt them, but you need to be more familiar with creating them, and bringing them to you."

"Why do I need to know so much?"

"You are going to have to face him one day, John. The Masked Man. Do you think he is going to go easy on you? He knows an infinite amount more than you do right now. You have to at least try to catch up before you will have a chance at defeating him," Howard responded. John agreed. At this point he wasn't sure how he would ever be able to win a fight against the Masked Man. "There are others you will need to protect yourself from. Axton wasn't the only one who was misled by his ego. There are many others who could find out a little bit about the other side, then do all they can to control it and to profit from it. They are people who don't wish to help anyone, just themselves. You will need to stop them. They could come to you anywhere, at any time, and you need to be ready," Howard explained to him. "I will send you back before morning every day so no one will know I am training you. You should carry on your old life, so no one gets suspicious. The Masked Man should leave you alone as long as you are not drawing attention to yourself. It will be easy to notice you if you do things that are out of the ordinary. It causes ripples in this world, through everyone who witnesses it. We have to start slow, open your hand, and create a red rubber ball."

John lifted his hand and closed his eyes, concentrating on making a rubber ball in his hand. He felt weight upon his hand and opened his eyes to find a rubber ball in his hand, but it was green instead of red. He must have been thinking of Mary Jane. John focused on the task again, and another ball appeared, just as not red as the first one, it was an even darker green.

"Clear your mind. Let go of your attachment. Don't want it to happen, know it is happening. It already happened. Believe in it and trust the universe. You have the connection, and the ability, you just need to understand it so that you can use it," Howard told him. John tried again and this time there was a single red ball in his hand. He smiled at his success until the ball started melting into a gooey liquid.

You're lucky that didn't happen with Axton, John's mind told him, or maybe that would have been a good thing. How much *did* you like being a hostage?

"JOHN! You are getting distracted. Let your thoughts go by, do not pay attention to them," Howard said, "let's try creating something more complex. Create a mobile phone. No, that is too complex to start out with, it would probably be easier to bring one from somewhere else. We will work on that too, and your control of energy. I know what happened when you first flew through the universe building power, and that will not do. We can't have you smashing coffee tables every time you travel through space." They continued on in this fashion for the rest of their time together, before John had to wake up in the morning. It was strange how time worked. The lesson always seemed to have ended right before his alarm went off. There was no time here, yet it always matched perfectly. John spent his time creating a variety of other things: flowers, rocks, hammocks, a small rubber ducky, and much more. Some of the items were sturdy, and others caught on fire. There was even one particularly memorable moment when he created a toilet brush that started singing the blues. John needed every bit of practice and training that he could get before he would be able to stand up to the Masked Man.

Chapter 17
Dinner & The Store

John woke up that morning feeling better than ever. His quality of sleep had gone up immensely even though he had spent most of the night awake, training on the beach in the other world. He was having breakfast with Mary Jane when the phone rang. It was his boss at the store calling to sarcastically ask John if he would be coming in for work today. With his whole world changed, you can imagine how little John wanted to go back to his normal life, especially working with such an imbecile, but Howard had told him to do normal things so that he wouldn't draw attention to himself. John told Mary Jane he would have to go to work. She took it better than he expected, I guess the part of people that gets angry is the same part that doesn't understand how the world works. Maybe he had been projecting his unwillingness upon her.

"It's okay," said Mary Jane, "I really should go see my parents. They are probably getting worried about me. I don't really know how long it has been since they saw me... it has been forever for me."

"It won't take very long. I am only scheduled until five today," said John. "It might even be a nice way for me to relax, by doing something ordinary. I'll miss you, babe." He kissed her as they left together. John drove Mary Jane to her parents house before he went to work. He was trying to keep a low profile and neither of them were that comfortable with sending themselves through space.

Upon entering the store, John was greeted by his boss with the usual, "We were going to have to call missing persons if you didn't get here soon." This time John just smiled, kind of happy to be back in his old life, only now knowing that none of it mattered. "Well, somebody is happy today," his boss said as John walked by.

"I really am," John said. "I met a girl." John knew his boss would understand, as that was a sufficient enough reason for any guy to be this happy.

"Well just wait until she asks you to marry her," his boss said with a laugh. "She'll get her hooks into you and hold on for dear life, ha ha. If you ask me you should be the one holding on to her."

John was still smiling, this was actually his boss being nice to him. As people started coming to John to cash out their orders, he noticed that he was on a roll. Everything was so perfect. He felt light and unburdened. There was not much he could do to keep from dancing to himself while he worked, which made more than one person laugh as they walked out of the building. John seemed to know everything people were going to say before they said it. He had their exact change ready before the computer had finished the orders.

"Wow, you really are good at your job son," an elderly man said to John as his transaction was completed.

John's boss came over to him. "I don't know what you are doing John, but everybody seems to love you today. Keep it up. At this rate you'll get a promotion by the end of the year. I'm glad something has finally gotten through to you."

John smiled and shook his head as his boss walked away. Damned if he was going to be stuck in this dead end job or the one his boss had. There was no work anymore, just existence. Everything was going to go the way he wanted it to now. Once he was strong enough to fight the

Masked Man, he would shape his world the way he wanted it, instead of the way everyone else wanted it for him. Anyone with the nerve to kidnap his girlfriend and try to kill him had it coming, he was thinking to himself, when he was interrupted.

"Excuse me, I think that one is no good," an elderly lady said to him gently. John looked down and saw a cantaloupe he had been running through the register melting and turning to mush before his very eyes.

"Oh dear, I thought I picked a good one," said the woman, adjusting her spectacles. She had no idea that it was because of John that the cantaloupe was falling apart. That wouldn't make any sense. He couldn't control it. Wherever his mind went, the energy followed. He still needed to learn to let go of his mind, and live beyond. His connection to the other side was getting stronger, and as it did, his mind was connecting with it as well. John called a runner to get a new cantaloupe for the woman.

"It's all right ma'am, we'll get another one for you." John's smile faded into a worried look. What if he did something much worse without meaning to, and ended up hurting someone? It had just been a cantaloupe this time but what if it had been something more significant? What if it was someone he loved, who said the wrong thing and made him cause this? He would have to talk to Howard about it, and do more meditating. John got through most of the day before something else happened. As he was handing a man his change, the coins started floating in his hand. A look of shock appeared on the man's face, but quickly changed back to normal.

"You know for a second there, I could swear those coins were floating! Boy the mind really plays tricks on you sometimes doesn't it?" said the man as he walked away from the register.

As John left to go home that day, his boss just stared at him, not sure what to say. The day had started off so brightly for John, and ended so poorly. When he got home he noticed Mary Jane sitting on the front steps.

"I hope you haven't been waiting long," he said to her.

"No, I knew you would be done at five, so I headed over a few minutes ago. I have some good ideas I want to discuss with you."

"You didn't have to stay out here, the door is unlocked. I don't have anything worth taking, and have secretly been hoping someone would break in and leave something more valuable."

Mary Jane knew he was kidding, but it was true that most of the material world had lost its value during their training. John raised his key to the door, but the door opened for him before he could put it in the lock. Luckily, Mary Jane didn't notice. John's mind was connecting and creating his thoughts in the material world. He had to watch everything he said from then on. It wasn't just his thoughts, even speaking would be created as truth onto this plane.

"I'll have to make a key for you," John said. "In the meantime there is a spare under the welcome mat. So what is it you wanted to talk about?" John asked as they walked into his house.

"Well, you know I want to do normal 'couple things' with you, since it has been so long since I've seen you, being trapped in the Chateau and all... I'm rambling aren't I?" Mary Jane asked him. She had been, but he asked her politely to continue without any acknowledgement of it. "Anyway, I do want to go to dinner and such with you, but I also love meditating with you, and thought of a really good idea." John nodded for her to keep going. "I think we should do yoga together," said Mary Jane.

"Okay," said John.

"I think, you know, with us doing all of these postures and everything anyway, why not do it with other people and see if we can learn anything from a real class," she continued, looking at John for approval for something he had already accepted. She was very excited about it, he could tell.

"That is a great idea. Find out when the classes are and we'll go check it out," John said to her. "I think we deserve a night off too though, I want to take you to dinner somewhere nice." Mary Jane was thrilled that he liked the idea, and on top of that she would get to go on a real date with him.

"I'll go get ready," Mary Jane said, heading to the bathroom. She didn't have a change of clothes or anything, but must have had enough to touch up her makeup or whatever it was that girls do, John thought. When Mary Jane walked out of the bathroom, John handed her a dozen roses that he had created. "Awww, you are so sweet, did you pick these up from the store? You did a good job of hiding them."

"I didn't buy them," said John. "I made them."

"What!" she said in disbelief. "That's incredible. We should meditate after dinner, I want to start learning things like that."

"It works differently for everyone," John said. "The book picks and chooses lessons when you are ready for them. Axton told me the first thing that the book showed him was a section on time."

"There is a section on time?" asked Mary Jane, "No way!"

"He said there was, I haven't seen it yet. Everything on this plane seems to be non-existent. All the rules of physics are moot if you can connect with the other side. Space, time, everything..."

"Do you think we could... bring people back from the dead?"

John was silent at this question. He didn't have an answer, at least not one that would be pleasing to think about. Death was so solid... how could anything change it? Especially for the better. If everything was meant to happen, then death followed the same logic, but could it ever be done? No. There was no point in thinking about it.

They drove to the restaurant, and were seated promptly. John sat across from Mary Jane at a small table for two. It was a very romantic restaurant with real candles on the tables, dimmed lights, and servers in elaborate clothing. John didn't go to places like this often, because he considered them above his pay grade. He could afford it now, because he could create money. Fresh, new, crisp hundred dollar bills would appear in his wallet at the very thought of it. John bought an expensive bottle of wine for the two of them, and a full three course meal with a dessert they both shared at the end, and coffee for two.

"This is the best date I've ever been on," said Mary Jane. It wasn't about the money. She had been on dates that had cost ten times as much, but John would never know that. "Something is just different about you. It's like I can't imagine my life without you." They had the bottle of wine packaged so they could take the rest home, and headed back to John's house.

When they got there, both of them collapsed onto the bed.

"I know you wanted to meditate with me, but I think I'm too full to do anything but lay here tonight."

"Ugh, me too. Let's just cuddle and go to sleep," she said, and they did.

Chapter 18
Jimmy's Story

Many months later, Jimmy was walking Mary Jane to her bedroom, as was now usual, but this time there was something that needed to come out. "Tell me the story of how you got trapped in The Library," said Mary Jane.

Jimmy paused for a moment with an awkward look on his face before speaking, "That is a very long story. Believe it or not, it was my choice to stay in The Library."

"Why would you willingly stay there?" Mary Jane asked him.

"Well there are a lot of reasons, let me start at the beginning. That is the best place to start you know, the beginning. Many a story has been ruined by starting at the wrong part, you know, but I suppose wherever you start becomes the beginning in a sense... I'm getting distracted.

To understand this story there are a few things you have to know. This story starts in 1725, when I was a young man about the age I look now. I spent all of my time at the State House Library. It was one of the first in the country. The idea fascinated me that all of that knowledge was free to the public. I would go there whenever I had spare time. Three years later in 1728, I met Victoria who would become my loving wife. Believe it or not, we even met at that library. We talked to each other about the books we had read, and were reading. It was incredible to find someone with the same passion for books that I had. Oh, she was an amazing woman. I loved her with all my heart.

It was a sad day for both of us when the State House caught fire. December 9, 1747. I remember it well. Victoria and I both stood outside of the burning building with tears in our eyes, helpless to save the books. We made it our personal mission to build up the biggest collection we could for the new library that was built a few years later. They even hired us both to work there. I knew everything there was to know.

We were the happiest married couple in the world for twenty more years until my wife developed polio, and was unable to walk. It hurt me so much to see her that way, frail and in pain," Jimmy continued. "That is when I met God. Ha ha, well maybe not *The* God, but he was God to us. He was a sharply dressed man with a dark goatee. I remember thinking how nice his outfit was. It was like nothing I had ever seen before, and nobody at that time had a goatee. There wasn't even a word for it back then. Sure there were wealthy people in Boston from time to time, but nobody looked anything like that. At the time I wouldn't have believed it if it hadn't happened to me.

He came to the library and told me he wanted to make a deal. He said he noticed my love of books and was touched by it. He himself had just built the biggest Library there would ever be. It seemed like a grand claim at the time, but now I know I should have believed him.

I asked him where it was and he just said, "Very far away." He told me he had a job for me there if I wanted it, but I couldn't start yet. He would give me all the money I needed but there was a catch. I would never be able to leave The Library.

I told him I would have to take my wife with me, but he said it would only be me. I was going to refuse, but there was more to the deal that he hadn't told me about yet. If I worked at his Library I would never grow any older. He said time worked differently there. Normally I would have been skeptical, but something about this man told me he was telling the truth. Even then, I would never want to live forever, even though there were enough books to last me all of eternity. I insisted that I take my wife with me, and he finally gave in, but there was still more he hadn't mentioned.

I wouldn't be able to start at The Library until the last day of my life, which is when he would come and get me. That is when he told me the real payment for my services: He was going to cure my wife. It's a shame, he told me, they were going to invent a vaccine for polio in about two hundred years and all of this could have been avoided. I didn't know how he knew that at the time, but I have come to understand a lot more after reading so much. The deal sounded too good to be true. I really didn't want the love of my life to spend an eternity in agony and suffering.

He gave me a slip of paper that was folded in half. "You can only use this once," he told me. "Read it out loud in front of your wife and she will be cured."

I took Victoria to the park to tell her the good news, that we would be able to save her and live in the world's largest library forever. She was so happy to hear it. There was nothing we wanted more than to spend our lives together learning. A book can take you so much farther than any other means of travel. I took out the slip of paper, ready to read it to her, when she told me to stop. There was a young boy who was being pushed around in a wheelchair. The boy didn't look good. He had the same disease, and he was much further along. By this point Victoria and I were in our sixties. She pointed at the boy, and looked deeply in my eyes. I knew at that moment that the choice was already made. I had to use the cure on that boy instead of her. We had already lived so long, and he was just getting started. I went over to the boy, and got down on my knee to talk to him.

"It's going to be all right," I told him. "I have a cure for you right here." I opened up the slip of paper and there was only one word. *The* word. "Apertambuxtion." I read it aloud to the boy and the color immediately returned to his face. The piece of paper burst into flames, and the word was lost from my memory for quite some time. He started smiling, and got up out of the wheelchair. The man who had been pushing him around in the wheelchair exclaimed that it was a miracle that his boy was cured. He had already given up hope for his son. The man thanked me profusely and asked me if there was anything he could do for me. He was a very wealthy man, but all of the money in the world would never amount to the life of his son. I told him that it was enough thanks that his son would live a long and full life. My wife and I both had tears in our eyes, knowing the sacrifice we had just made to save the boy, and for the second chance he had been given.

Three years later my wife died. It is the hardest thing a man has to go through, to lose someone so close. Losing her was to lose a part of me as well. I took solace in knowing that she died happy, having saved a young boy's life in place of her own. I did everything I could to make her comfortable during the previous years. The man and his son were at her funeral, he even paid for all of the expenses without my knowing it.

On my eightieth birthday the fancy dressed man with the goatee came to me, and told me it was time. I nodded and got up to follow him. He gave me a slight nod and the next thing I knew we were both outside of The Library in a small hallway. I wondered how big it could be since it was such a small hallway, then he opened the door. It is incredible you know. Every book ever written is in that Library. It has to be the most important thing in history. I cried when I saw it knowing how great it would have been for Victoria to be there with me. The man seemed to know things without me even telling him. He gave his sincere condolences for Victoria and told me that it was the only way it could have happened. This is why he said I would have to do it alone. He knew I would use the cure on the boy instead of my wife, because that was how the universe wanted it. I wouldn't have been able to live with myself knowing I condemned that boy to an early grave.

The man told me people would visit from time to time, and that I would be able to leave one day. He showed me the private room with only one book in it, and told me that when someone comes asking for it, I would be able to regain my youth and return to the world. He showed me around the whole Library including the personal quarters where I would live. He told me there was no need to eat or sleep, but if I wanted to, I could. He said any food I wanted would be there when I was craving it. That would have seemed impossible to me if I hadn't already seen so much.

After he left, I wondered if I could find anything out about the book, but when I opened it up there was nothing but blank pages. Every year an envelope appeared on my desk with pictures of the boy who had been saved, and his family. He was already in his thirties, and had a family with three kids. I saw his whole life go by, generation after generation of his family going through the cycle of life and death. After many generations there were two men left. One of them was the man who took me to The Library and the other got married. His wife got pregnant with a daughter and they planned on naming her Mary Jane. That little girl is you. So long ago I saved a boy's life and you are here because of it. It was meant to be. You were the one who saved me from The Library. It had to be this way. I wish Victoria could be here to see what she created."

Jimmy was crying at this point. Mary Jane was hot with the mind blowing revelation at the end of his story. Everything in the universe fit together so perfectly. It was unbelievable. It also meant her uncle was still alive... wherever it is that he was... or *when*ever. "I think you've had enough of my stories for tonight young lady. Thank you for being so kind and listening to me," Jimmy said as he got up to leave.

"No, thank you. For making that sacrifice. I wouldn't be here if it weren't for you. Thank you Jimmy," Mary Jane said. He smiled and nodded with tears still running down his face. He suddenly looked a lot older and more fragile. Jimmy was not the monster he had appeared to be at the coffee shop and there was so much that John and Mary Jane had yet to find out. Time continued to pass with Mary Jane stuck at the Chateau with the Master, Jimmy, and all of the followers. With practice, sections of the book continued to open in her mind. Every so often the Master would have Mary Jane come to him so he could teach her new things. She needed to be prepared to do anything when she went back in time to save John.

Chapter 19
Conflicted

It had been months since John and Mary Jane lived a semi-normal life together. John had quit his job after he used his new power to fill his bank account. He would never have to work a dead end job again. He and Mary Jane could live happily ever after once he killed the Masked Man who had kidnapped her. John took it upon himself as his personal mission to get revenge. That night, when Howard brought him to the beach, John was in for a surprise. Howard was extremely angry with him.

"What is wrong with you?" he shouted at John. "I give you these powers and tell you to be inconspicuous and this is how you repay me?" John was uncomfortable. He knew this was going to happen eventually. "You are using the power for your own benefit! Putting millions of dollars in your bank account and quitting your job! You're not supposed to draw attention to yourself. Have you learned anything at all? It was one thing to create flowers for your girlfriend and take her out to dinner but this has gotten out of hand. You are completely overtaken by your mind aren't you? Do you even know why you are doing this? Don't you understand money is worthless? You are letting it take over your life. All of this material garbage is going to do it's job and keep you distracted from what is real," Howard was giving him the lecture of a lifetime.

"What good is all of this power, if I can't even live comfortably?" John shouted back at him. "I have to live like a slave to the stupid material world? How is that fair? I can do anything with this, and damned if I'm not going to enjoy my own life!"

"Power!?! Power! You think this is power? It is nothing! You are greedy! Your ego thinks that it can control and possess! Haven't I taught you anything? None of it is real," Howard yelled back at him. "This is the last time I bring you here. You have failed me! Get out of my sight!"

"I never want to see your face again old man," John shouted back at him, being as hurtful as he could. "I hope you are stuck here alone forever!" John immediately regretted saying it when he saw the pain in Howard's eyes. He started to apologize but the damage was already done.

Howard was trying to gain his strength back from that blow, "You've gone too far, John. I was only ever here to help you. If you keep this up you're going to get exactly what you deserve."

"I'm so..." John started to speak, but he was already back in his bed with Mary Jane when the word finally came out of his mouth. "Sorry." To make matters worse, when John finally managed to get back to sleep, the Masked Man came to him a dream.

"You did it John, you managed to push away another person who cared about you," the Masked Man said taunting him. "You are weak. You alienate everybody, it's no wonder you have been alone so much of your life."

"Shut up," John yelled at him.

"At this rate, I won't have to do anything," said the Masked Man. "You will do it all for me!"

"Agghhhhh," John screamed lunging toward the Masked Man in anger. The Masked Man held up his hand and John was thrown to the floor.

"Child's play. You really haven't learned anything. You think you'll be able to face me! That's a laugh," said the

Masked Man. "You don't deserve to have such a faithful girl by your side. That's why I took her from you."

"Oh you just wait," said John. "I'm going to get you. I'm coming for you and there is nothing you can do to stop me." John woke up, and it was now morning. He was angrier than ever.

That is it, John thought. I know everything I need to know. Tomorrow I am going to kill the Masked Man. The next day Mary Jane noticed that John was tense. "Is something wrong?" she asked him.

"No, I am fine. Look, I need you to leave for the day. There is something I have to do," John said. He was hurting her by being so distant. Mary Jane agreed because she could tell it was no use talking to him. She kissed him before walking out the door. John put his head in both of his hands and groaned. He was becoming a monster. As soon as he got back from the Chateau with the good news he would make it up to her. John clenched his teeth and closed his eyes. When he opened them again he was at the Chateau.

As Mary Jane was walking away from the house she stopped dead in her tracks. "Oh no," she said out loud, "he is going to kill him." Mary Jane ran back into the house but John was already gone.

Chapter 20
Starting Things Up

The Master told Mary Jane that the time was approaching that she would have to leave. "If you have any unfinished business here you have three days to wrap it all up." That night Jimmy came to Mary Jane's room once again. He had in his hands, the book. It was a large book with gold letters reading, "Apertambuxtion."

"I am glad the Master gave you notice before you left. We have to get this book back in time to give it to John," said Jimmy.

"This is what started everything. Where did you get it?" Mary Jane asked him.

"It is the copy from The Library," Jimmy said. "You gave it to me at The Library when we escaped. Don't worry, it never really leaves you once you connect with it." Jimmy took out a small bag of chocolates as well. "If you give John one of these, he'll be able to do what he needs to, in order to see the path he will follow," said Jimmy. "I will arrive shortly after you and pretend I am trying to kill him."

Mary Jane and Jimmy did some of the postures and started meditating. Pretty soon they were both standing outside of the store where John worked, on the very day they needed to be there. "You go in first," Jimmy said. "Then I will come in and start throwing around energy."

"Okay," said Mary Jane. She walked into the store, and it became the first time John saw her. It looked like he was holding his breath. Mary Jane was impressed that John was that attracted to her. She really did mean that much to him, even when he didn't know her. That's the way the universe wants it, she thought to herself. She stood there for a little while wondering if he was going to say anything or if she should just stand there awkwardly.

"Can I help you find anything today?" John finally spoke to her.

"John," she said trying to sound mysterious. "You know why I am here. It's time for change." John looked spacey. He was staring at everything like it was the most interesting thing in the world. If she didn't know him, Mary Jane might be freaked out by this behavior. Mary Jane waved her hand in front of his face but he was unresponsive. She walked back out of the store and talked to Jimmy. "Jimmy, he is just standing there with a blank look, I think it's time for you to go in."

Jimmy walked into the store to find John's boss yelling at him. Although this wasn't the John who saved Jimmy from The Library with Mary Jane, Jimmy still felt some sort of responsibility and pride for John, so he shoved John's boss out of the way with more force than he probably should have used in this dimension. Jimmy then remembered the real reason he was there, and started walking toward John with his hands held up menacingly. He hoped his acting was believable. Jimmy started throwing energy near John, not trying to hit him, but making it look like he was. Then John disappeared completely. Jimmy quickly helped John's boss on to his feet, and erased the destruction he had wrought.

When Jimmy left the building, he told Mary Jane that it had gone well, but part of him had been worried John would wake up at any time, and throw him across the room. Jimmy knew that John was dangerous and had to trust that John didn't know that. After all, it wasn't this John, even though it was the same person, was it? They heard a loud noise, and noticed that John was back in the store again. "It's time to send him out of here," said Mary Jane. "He told me that he saw me right after this. Can you send us both somewhere else?" Jimmy nodded and threw a ball of energy at John to throw him to another location, and waved a hand at Mary Jane. They both disappeared. Jimmy was left standing there for a brief moment before he disappeared as well. If witnessed by anyone it would be played off as a trick of the mind or a practical joke. Maybe they wouldn't have seen anyone standing there in the first place.

Mary Jane found herself in a dark room all alone for a few minutes before John appeared. She didn't know where it was, but it seemed to have gone how it was supposed to. The only way it could. She remembered some of the words John had mentioned about this moment when they were in the coffee shop together. "It's okay John. You did it. The energy was used to bring you here instead of spewing your atoms into the atmosphere," said Mary Jane. John opened his eyes and put down his hands. "I don't know how you knew to do that, but you did it just in time," she said.

"I don't know what is going on," John said.

"It's okay, everything will come in time. Most of it you have to remember on your own, but I will help teach you what I can," she replied. " My name is Mary Jane." Mary Jane knew this probably sounded confusing and ominous, but that seems to be what the universe kept making happen, so who was she to disagree?

"My name is John," said John.

"We already know that John," said Mary Jane who then remembered that he didn't know that yet. "It's okay John, I am here to explain it to you. Well. What I am allowed to at least." Mary Jane had a hard time looking

117

away from him. He was still the cute innocent guy she had fallen in love with in the first place, even if he didn't know it yet. It was going to be difficult to explain all of this to someone who didn't even know there was anything beyond, but Mary Jane knew that she had done it already in the past, and that she shouldn't be worrying about it. She decided to appeal to his emotional self. They both had a connection, and that might be the easiest way to go through with this conversation. "We only have tonight for me to tell you all that I can John," said Mary Jane. "You'll have to trust me. I don't know if there is anything I can say right now to make this easier, but somewhere in your heart, in your soul, you can feel that we have a connection. You know me. I can't tell you how I know it, it is a feeling I have that I can see is budding inside of you as well. It is instinctual. It's because time does not progress as you think it does. Everything between us has already happened, even though the possibility didn't even exist a few hours ago. For now I need you to trust me because I know a lot more than you do about this and I want you to know how meaningful it is to both of us." Mary Jane took out the chocolate. "Let me give you something to help you relax John," she said to him handing him the chocolate.

"Chocolate is supposed to help me relax? How about lighting some candles and playing romantic music too," said John half-sarcastically.

"It's not just chocolate you goof. There is something inside of it that will help open your understanding. The chocolate is just there to mask the taste," she said to him.

"Well, so much for not taking candy from strangers," John said just before eating the piece of chocolate. John got that weird look on his face again. Mary Jane hadn't tried the chocolate, so she was just guessing what John was feeling at this point. "What did you give me?" John asked.

Mary Jane tried to explain everything to him as briefly as she could, "All right John. Here comes the hard part," Mary Jane began. "Some of this is going to be difficult for you to understand. I pray that it will work. I need you to relax and let go while I explain what I can. First, the world is not as we see it. I already mentioned that time has already happened, it is all one, we see it all at once, not linearly like you do. That is just a mental block. It is one of the hardest things to overcome, and we don't have enough time to work on it now. The most important thing we need to focus on is you John. Well, not you as John, but you as what you really are. We are all part of one giant energy system. When they say energy cannot be created or destroyed they are right, but it can easily be relocated, manipulated, and connected. A long time ago we could manipulate it freely, but then something came along and blocked all access we had to control the universe. Someone decided it would be better if we didn't know anything about it. They wanted us to only see part of the picture and to struggle through life. That is where most people are. Stuck. It's like they are looking at a two-way mirror and only see one side of it. This knowledge started leaking out slowly into the world. It is impossible to contain something so universal. In places with suffering, it is strongest and easiest to see. You hear all kinds of stories of people lifting cars and doing impossible things. They are all possible. We just have to believe in it or the mind will stop us. The limits are of our own perception. The world we see is not the world that is really there. Are you starting to feel it John? You look like you're enjoying it. That's good. Now it's time for the harder part. You have to let go of everything you believe. Nothing here is real. All of it can be changed, altered, and adapted by you. You have to forget about science. There is no gravity. All of the laws we have been given were put there to hold us back. Nothing is the color that you see or even in the same place. You can see the entire history and future of everything, but I am getting ahead of myself. We need to start this simply. Hold out your hand. Okay. Do you see any of the glowing?" Mary Jane noticed that John was connecting at this point and doing his best to deal with this new sensation.

"My hands. Are they still mine?" John asked her.

"Are they still whose, John? They are still part of a body, did they ever really belong to anything? You see them as your hands, but they are no one's hands. There are no hands. There is no you. Everything is the same, it is all one big existence. I know it is hard to understand. The hand is as much mine as it is yours," she said. Mary Jane flexed her fingers and John saw his own fingers do the same action. "Let go of your attachment. None of it is real," she said. John moved his fingers and watched as her fingers did the same. "Now you are getting it," she said, noticing her own fingers moving at his command. It was coming easy for him. Mary Jane could see through John's eyes as well as her own, but the her that was seeing as him, was not Mary Jane, it was the universe.

It was time to test him. "Think of an object," said Mary Jane, "anything will do, but it has to be something you can hold in your hand. I want you to imagine that you are holding it. I want you to bring that object to your hand. Ignore anything that tells you it isn't possible." A small stuffed cat appeared in John's hand. Mary Jane was surprised because she recognized it from her childhood. "Why did you create that?" asked Mary Jane, backing up slightly. "How did you... know? John," she continued, "it really is you. I can see it. When I was a young girl, I had a stuffed cat just like this," said Mary Jane, "I took it with me everywhere, but one day I lost it. It seemed like some unseen force took it away from me. You brought it here John. That is the same cat I had as a little girl." Mary Jane looked down for a minute, trying to move past this because she didn't think John was ready to understand it.

"What happened to your stuffed cat?" asked John.

"I found it a few moments later," she said, "it was like it had been there all along." The cat disappeared from John's hand. Mary Jane knew she would have to speed things up. "We're running out of time," she said to him. "Well... in this linear progression of it. It's already been four hours," said Mary Jane. She took out the book to give him. "Everything you need to know is in here. Take this book." She handed it to him. In a few seconds the book was gone, molding itself into John's energy. "The sections will open as you need them," said Mary Jane. "I have faith in you. It is not going to be easy, and you are the only one who can do it. Goodbye John. I will see you again when we are meant to. It is sooner than you know," she said. John slowly faded away until he was gone. Mary Jane stood there wondering when Jimmy would pull her back to the Chateau. It didn't take long. She was back in her room with Jimmy in a matter of minutes.

"I still have to get used to traveling that way," Mary Jane said.

"You may never get used to it," Jimmy said, "it still bugs me sometimes too. I think we did it. Everything should be in place now."

"Yes," said Mary Jane, "it was so weird seeing him like that wasn't it? I just wanted him to know everything."

"It certainly was," said Jimmy. "I had almost forgotten too, when I pushed that guy out of the way."

Chapter 21
The Beginning of The End

When the time came, the Master called her to the main hall. "Before I send you back he said to her, I have to tell you that I know you and Jimmy gave the book to John and started all of this."

"We had to," Mary Jane started to say, defending her actions.

"It's okay," said the Master. "It had to be done. I wanted to thank you for being here with me all of this time. I know it wasn't the easiest thing to do, but it had to be done. I hope you understand it all now."

"It is the only way it could have been," said Mary Jane.

"Exactly. One more thing before you go," said the Master, "who do you think wrote the book?" Mary Jane looked at him puzzled, she had no idea where the book came from. For all she could imagine it probably created itself. "I wrote it," said the Master smiling, "well, created it at least. It came through me from the other side." Mary Jane only had a second to look amazed before there was a flash and she was back at the Chateau on the day John was unfreezing the statue of Axton.

Right after the Master sent Mary Jane back in time, John appeared in the main hall to face the Master. Jimmy stood in front of him to protect the Master from John, but the Master told him it was all right, he could stand down. "There is only one way this can end, John," said the Master.

"That's right," said John, "I am here to kill you. You are going to pay for what you did." John started throwing energy at the Master. The Master blocked his attacks and threw his own at John. John narrowly missed the attacks, marble from the floor flew up into the air around him as the Master's energy tore through the Chateau. Things seemed like they were happening in slow motion. His heart was beating fast and he was losing control. John got close enough to the Master that they were throwing fists at each other. With one final scream, John shoved his hand against the Master's chest and threw everything he could at him blindly. The Master collapsed to his knees, and fell over dying. John stood over him spewing out hatred with every heaving breath.

Mary Jane appeared at the Chateau just in time to witness the final violent blow. "Noooooo!" she screamed, and ran over to the dying Master.

The Master spit up a little bit of blood and he laughed. "This is how it had to be," he said. "This is how it always had to be."

"John," Mary Jane said with a cry. "How could you do this? Why didn't you talk to me first?" John was shocked that Mary Jane was taking the Master's side after he had kidnapped her. "Oh John," she said with tears streaming down her face, "you shouldn't have. You don't know what you've done." She was crying and holding the Master's head in her lap. "I'm so sorry."

The Master coughed again and said to her, "Take off my mask. It is time to show him." Mary Jane gently lifted the mask off of his face and John was filled with a sense of dread when he realized who it was.

The face under the mask was his own face staring back at him. "He is you, John. *He* is who you are going to become," said Mary Jane. John was the Master. He had always been the Master, the most powerful, the most connected.

"No," John said horrified, "No . . ."

The Master mustered up all the energy he could to smile one last smile at John, "I forgive you John. It had to be this way. After all... you are going to be me. That is your punishment." The Master, who was now revealed to be John himself, gasped one final gasp and died. Mary Jane broke down completely. John went over to her but she pushed him away.

"No! Don't touch me. You are a monster!" John knew he had made the biggest mistake of his life. He was mortified. Jimmy stood by shaking his head and people started filing into the main hall to see what had happened. They formed a circle around John once again, staring at him silently.

"I didn't know..." John said. "I didn't know." For John, time stopped and the book opened up to him once again with "Section 4, Time." The information for manipulating and traveling through time came flooding into his brain. John knew he had to get away. As the followers got closer to him John shut his eyes and took himself out of there and into the past. The Chateau was quiet except for the sounds of Mary Jane crying as the followers stood watching her in silence.

"I'm so sorry," Jimmy said to her. "I don't know why he wanted it this way."

"I should have told him sooner," Mary Jane said sniffing. "Oh John, how could you do this? We're supposed to be the good guys."

Chapter 22
Good & Bad is Relative

This was the first time John had traveled through time intentionally. It was not very different from space, except that it was more disorienting. You just had to assume you were where you wanted to be when you got there. It's not like your wristwatch would turn backwards or anything, it would just be wrong if you got somewhere and it wasn't the same time. Not to mention the date. So John did the first cliché thing he could when he got there: he asked someone what year it is. Of course, they thought he was joking and wouldn't give him an answer. One man went so far as to discuss the philosophical meaning of time and that it was all man made anyway so really there was no year for it to be. That man didn't know how close to the truth he had been in that passing moment of observation.

Luckily for John, it was one of those time periods that still had newspapers. He was exactly where he wanted to be, and should have trusted that in the first place. John hated himself. Not just for what he was going to be, but for who that made him become. He knew that if he wasn't able to control his powers, he was going to hurt more people, so in an erratic state of mind he had made the decision to go back to his own childhood... to make sure he never *could* hurt anyone. John closed his eyes and concentrated on what his bedroom was like as a child. In just a brief moment, he was standing over a crib with a young baby version of himself looking at him inquisitively. "All I have to do is put a pillow over your face for a few minutes," John said quietly to the baby, more to himself, in order to realize the seriousness of what he was about to do. It was one thing to kill an older more powerful version of himself, but this innocent baby version of him didn't stand a chance. This would mean that none of it ever happened. That's what John liked about it. Mary Jane could live her own life and be happy without him, and he would never have to struggle through all of this.

John was standing over the crib thinking so intently that he didn't notice the two people who had entered the room. "He's going to hurt our baby," a woman's voice came. John was grabbed from behind and was struggling with the man whose arms were wrapped around him. John was fighting the grasp when his mind went to a place it shouldn't have. A dangerous place. The man was thrown to the ground gasping his last few breaths. The lack of control John had over his power just caused him to kill his own father. His mother stared at him horrified, screaming, "get away from my baby! What do you want from us! Help! Help! Somebody help me, don't let him hurt my baby!" John was filled with panic. He had completely lost control again. John stared blankly at his mother, starting to understand. This is why she was afraid of him when he visited her in the future. John was the reason his father was dead, and that his mother was crazy. He was the reason that young John was going to have to spend his childhood in an orphanage. His mother's crying and shouting was piercing his soul with pain as he slowly turned his head away from her.

John closed his eyes and disappeared from the room. He had done it wrong, again. As John left the baby version of himself behind, another figure took his place in the room. John's mother was still screaming about her baby while there was a bright light the size and shape of a doorway that appeared in the middle of the room. The man who had appeared there lifted the body of John's father and stepped through the light which promptly disappeared leaving John's mother with a story that would get her locked up and a screaming baby who would grow up alone.

John was getting stronger, and still had no control over his power. He needed someone to teach him. He knew he needed Howard to teach him, but Howard would never agree after their last argument and when he saw what had just happened. That is why John chose to go where he did next. He closed his eyes and then opened them at the Temple, before it had burned down. After all, he was the Masked Man now, and he had to follow in his footsteps. John used his powers to change his clothes from jeans and a t-shirt to a modest dressing fit for someone who would be spending the next few years in the Temple. He stood there for a second looking at his hands, where appeared the mask he was to wear until the day of his death, by his own hand. John took a deep breath and put on the mask. He walked into the Temple, straight toward Howard. John bowed in front of Howard who was sitting cross-legged with his hands on his knees and closed eyes. Howard was aware of the presence. "You are very strong," Howard said to him. "You have very much potential, but also sorrow, and a certain darkness that you are hiding. Why do you wish to be a student here?"

"I need guidance," John said. "I made the wrong decisions in the past and I need someone to lead me down the right path. I am having trouble controlling what I do and what my mind creates."

"Ah, yes," Howard said, "I see. You have broken the biggest rules there are, young one. Do not worry, it is not as bad as you think it is. The idea of good and bad are all a creation of the mind. They are what the mind uses to distract you into thinking you had a choice in the matter. I will allow you to be my student, but you must follow everything I say, exactly to the word."

John bowed before him once again. "It would be my honor," John said.

"It would be my honor as well," Howard said. "I heard from the other side that this has been a long time coming. Fate has decided long ago that I would be your teacher and this is how it must be. Now go, sit next to our other new students. They are father and son you know. What a bond they must have." John walked over to the new students who were cross-legged with their eyes shut. One was older and one was younger. Then it hit John like a ton of bricks, it was Axton and Jeff The Cleaner. They had been here as well.

A vision flooded into John's head of Jeff talking to Howard, "Please accept my son and I as your dedicated students. He has a good heart, but I am afraid of what he might become. He has a greed for power, and I am afraid he might hurt someone. Please teach him humility, and to control his urges." Even from a young age, Jeff feared that Axton might be a danger to the world.

In the vision, Howard's face had a small but noticeable frown as he spoke, "I will take you both as students. I fear it may not be enough, but this is what must be. It has already been done." Howard had a firm grasp of how time worked and didn't work. He could already see some of what would happen before it did.

The vision ended, and Howard spoke to John who was just getting into position. "If you are finished daydreaming, our first lesson is silence."

"Oh, silence! This will be fun," Jeff said very enthusiastically to Axton, who was already sitting seriously.

Howard continued his lesson, "Sit quietly and listen. Hear everything. Hear what is there, hear what is not there. Do not listen or interpret any sound or what it could be, just accept what it is. It must be heard whether the sound enters your ears or not. Sound is simply another form of energy that distracts you from the beyond. When all is gone from your head, you will hear the sound of silence. The stillness of silence is the most peaceful sound in the universe. Let go of the sounds and start to hear silence. Let go of all of it, including my voice. Let it come and pass without touching your mind. Walk without touching the ground, hear without there being a sound. We will practice for three hours today, starting now." Howard stopped speaking. John needed lessons like this. Simple lessons. The book had skipped some of the easier but more important steps in his process. Learning to control his senses was the first step toward being able to control himself. John could turn steel into mush and jump through time like a time traveling frog, but he hadn't taken the time to appreciate sound and silence. The silence between every sound. That is what made sound exist, the silence, dualistically. He had never known how noisy his world had become, including the very voice in his head that he was supposed to be observing.

After a while, John was hearing everything, but not listening. Sounds started to have no meaning. The sounds would exist and hit his ears, then pass by without being interpreted. For a second John heard his own breath like the ocean roaring, before it passed from meaning along with the rest. "Ahhhhhhh," the universe let out a giant sigh in John's mind like all the pressure had been released from his existence. Then for the first time, silence came to John with a gentle humming. The sound of the universe. John's existence flooded all over the world and to the other side. Everything felt perfect. It was all exactly as it had to be. Peaceful and comfortable. It would be easy to get lost in this feeling for anyone who ever had stress in their life.

The comfortable silence was broken by Axton who stood up and said, "This is stupid, how can someone hear silence?" Jeff tried to pull Axton back down next to him, but Axton shook him off and ran out of the room.

"Axton," Jeff yelled getting up to go after him.

Howard raised a hand and said, "It will not be necessary. Let him go. He needs room for himself to exist."

John didn't know how long he had been at the Temple. There were no clocks or calendars there. Just the sun rising and setting. He had been practicing every day along with the other students, and pretty soon he was practicing the most advanced techniques. John didn't like to talk with the other students because he wasn't really sure that he was even supposed to be here at this point, and thought it could disrupt something in the future. He was still full of shame from the accidents he had instigated and didn't want to see who he had become... who the Masked Man had turned him into... he couldn't blame the Masked Man anymore. For one thing, it was himself, but for another, the choices he made were his own, not someone else's. John was afraid to talk to other people because he would see himself in them, and it reminded him of what he was now. He carried on his duties responsibly and became more and more powerful. Howard gave him the name of Adamant One, as his identity had yet to be known, and because of the conviction he showed for keeping on his mask and studying diligently. John told them he must wear the mask to cover his own shame for what he had done, which was more true than he cared to admit to himself. They agreed to let him wear it for his own sake, and because it would help him to let go of his identity with himself as being somebody, instead of one who is everything.

Chapter 23
The Creation

With his newly discovered connective powers, John knew what he had to do to bring it all full circle. He left time and this dimension, then used the other side to create new spaces at the beginning of time as we know it. From where there was nothing, the beach where Howard would be stranded was created out of John's own will. In another space, the Chateau appeared, complete with all of the bronze sculptures, but one. In another spot, The Library. These places had to come from somewhere, John thought to himself, and now he knew the answer. John was living up to the title he would soon earn, the Master. When he got back to the Temple, John meditated for a long time. He had one more thing to create. In front of him in empty space, there appeared the leather binding of a book, then the pages filling it. It was a large book with gold letters reading, "Apertambuxtion." The book was glowing and humming as it was given life and everything it would need to perform it's task. John's connection to the other side allowed him to create it in such a way that it was more powerful than even he knew. It had a way about it that kept it connected to the other side. It was a miracle that such a thing could be brought over, an entire gateway in this form. There was a flash and the book disappeared. Frozen in time at the coffee shop, the book that had just been created appeared in front of Mary Jane.

John went outside to the edge of the forest to find Howard. "I need your help," John said to him.

"Ahh, come and sit with me," Howard said peacefully. "What is it you need, Adamant One?"

"This is going to be a lot to handle," John said to him.

"I will do anything I can for you Adamant One, you are my greatest student. Remember that difficulties are in your mind. All that we are meant to do, will be done. Understand as well that you will do many good things in your lifetime to balance out whatever it is that brought you here."

"Thank you," said John. "If you are truly connected with the other side, I will not have to explain very much of this to you. For the rest of it, you will have to trust me. I have been through time and seen what must be. There is someone from my journey who must help me to put things into place, but I must not be known to him and cannot appear before him in a mask if he is to be convinced to help me."

"You want me to talk to him for you," said Howard. "What is it I will need to say to him?"

"His wife is dying of Polio," John said. "I need you to give him the cure in order to convince him to stay at The Library I have created. It is the largest Library there is, and it always needs someone there to take care of it. His name is James. He and his wife are very fond of books and it would make them both happy to be part of this."

"You created *The* Library," Howard said in amazement. "I thought it was just a myth that such a place existed!"

"Yes," said John, "I created The Library, but it already was, it just had to be brought into existence. There are some other things I need you to know for this to work. You must first try to convince James of staying there any way you can. The last resort will be the cure for his wife. That is the only thing that will convince him to go in the end, but he must know all there is to know before he becomes The Librarian. In this Library is a copy of every book that has ever existed. Time does not pass the same way there. Whoever is in The Library will not grow older. There will be no need to eat or sleep, but the option is available if one would so choose.

James is to be taken there on the last day of his life, which is why he will be more willing to go with you. He will want to take his wife with him. You can tell him that is okay, but the cure you give him is going to be given to someone else instead at the request of his wife. James will be in The Library alone. I will then take you to the day before he dies, and you must escort him to The Library, which I will assist you with. I will have to send you through space and time using my connection to the other side. You must also tell him about the private collection. There is a copy of a book that contains all the power in the universe. He is to keep it safe until someone comes asking about it. He will know who it is when the time comes, and on that day he will be able to leave The Library."

"Send me through space and time? That is a lot to manage," Howard said. "I will do it for you, Adamant One because I know you have changed and what you ask of me is for the best of everyone. I trust that with the training I have given you, that you are acting more wisely than you did before you came here."

"I am," said John. Howard's clothes changed to the fancy ones James described when he told Mary Jane the story of the strange man who had offered him the job at The Library. "Now brace yourself," John said to Howard. "We are about to travel through time."

Chapter 24
Back to The Temple

When they got back to the Temple, John continued studying under Howard's guidance, although Howard now knew that this was no ordinary student and that all of his teachings would never amount to half of what John could accomplish. There had never been such a powerful being. Soon enough, the book had shown John everything it had to show him. Although the information was still in his head, the book itself appeared in his lap while he was meditating. This was the first time John had seen it since Mary Jane had handed it to him while he was eating the chocolate. John gave the book to Howard, someone who would keep it safe. The power of the book in the wrong hands... John didn't want to think about it. When Howard took the book, it didn't interface with him. It acted like a normal book. The book seemed to have a consciousness of its own. The decisions it made to connect with people was a decision it would make, not one you could. "I am amazed at your progress, Adamant One," Howard said to him. "When you came to me you had no awareness of your own self. Now you stand before me handing me this book that you say is a most powerful device. It was a responsible choice for you to give it to me to protect, and it is a sign that you have become more conscious of what is right. I am proud of you, Adamant One. You are my best student." Howard bowed and John responded in kind before going back to his practice. During the whole conversation, Axton had been standing outside of the doorway listening. He had to get his hands on that book.

Less than a week later, Howard came to John in a state of panic. "Adamant One, the book! Someone has taken the book." John wasn't surprised by this. He didn't have to connect with the other side to remember that Axton told him his teacher gave him the book. It turns out he had been lying. Surprise. Axton had stolen the book. It wasn't time to get it back yet though.

"If someone has taken the book, that is how it was supposed to be," said John.

"How can you be calm about this?" Howard asked. "This isn't how it is supposed to be! That book is dangerous, we have to find it!" Howard and John had switched roles of teacher and student at this point as John was now the one trying to help Howard level out his energy, while Howard was out of control. Howard called all of the students and teachers to search the premises but the book could not be found. John knew where it was. He could smell it. Axton had it. Axton wasn't hiding it, the book was no longer on this plane, it had melded with Axton as it had decided. Howard did not inform the rest of the crowd why the book was so important. His credibility was questioned on this day, which was the ultimate reason he was later left out of the decision to banish one of his students.

Axton started gaining power. He was learning more than the other students. He could make it snow at will and turn French fries into onion rings, which he could have found out if they had French fries at the Temple. Axton looked through time, but what he saw was clouded by what his mind wanted. It created for him a false version of the future that was shaped by his mind instead of what was to be. As far as he could tell, he was going to get everything he wanted. All the power in the world at his fingertips. The ecstasy he felt was overwhelming when he thought about it. Axton thought himself to be invincible at this point.

Everyone was worried, seeing Axton so powerful and having no way to stop him. When he was confronted by a group of students who had banded together to stop him, without approval of the leaders, Axton broke down the final barrier that was keeping him at the Temple. The students watched in horror as their leader tried to fight Axton and was quickly drained of all his energy, leaving a pile of ash and a hungry Axton staring at them, laughing madly. There was a secret meeting between the elders and teachers (excluding Howard). They decided it was their responsibility to send Axton away somewhere he wouldn't be able to hurt anyone. With their power combined, they would be able to send him to a secret world where he could live out his days in peace and solitude. Axton's father begged them to be sent as well, but they didn't have enough combined energy to send more than one person. They were using an ancient enchantment that could only be used once.

Not everything quite made sense to John at this point. He knew that Axton used to have the book. He also knew from Howard's memory that the Masked Man was the one they tried to banish. John knew of their plan to banish Axton so he decided to get the book back himself. If Axton was banished with the book, it would negate everything. He could come right back. Banishing Axton sounded like a good idea to John, maybe he could avoid some of his struggle. John went to Axton's room and told him he had to stop or they were going to send him away.

"I can't let that happen," said Axton. "Thank you for being my only friend here. If it makes you feel any better, please know that I really am sorry for this." Axton grabbed John by the arm, which quickly filled with excruciating pain as John felt his energy being sucked away, but it shot through Axton like a lightning bolt and kept on coming until Axton screamed in pain, "Aghh!"

"What is wrong with you?" Axton yelled at him, "who are you!" John gasped for air at the sudden shift in energy that had come with his connection to the other side. If anything, he had also gained power from the experience. His connection to the other side was not so easily broken. John had also exchanged energy with Axton. A gateway allows for things to go both ways. In his hands was the book which had come to him through Axton when the connection was open. "Give that back," exclaimed Axton, but by the time he had reached John, the book was already gone.

John had put it some place safe. He sent it forward in time to the Chateau where Jimmy would later take it to give to Mary Jane to then pass on to a younger version of John.

"Oh, you're going to pay for that," said Axton. John was getting dizzy from the change in energy and his vision started to fade. In just a moment, John was on the ground unconscious while Axton stood over him. Axton put John in his bed where they would assume Axton was sleeping that night. They would take John away instead of Axton. "The only way they will believe he is me, is if I wear the mask as well," Axton thought to himself. He had learned enough from the book to create his own copy of the mask.

Wearing a copy of the mask, Axton went to the elders and told them his version of the story, "Axton attacked me! He tried to kill me and something happened. He ended up having the same appearance I do. We have to get him out of here now!" Coming from the Adamant One, the story was unquestioned. They quickly headed to Axton's room where they grabbed John, who they believed to be Axton, and carried him outside to be exiled. John had been woken up when they grabbed him, but remembered what was to happen next from the memory Howard had showed him, so he didn't resist being tied up by the angry mob. Howard ran from where he had been meditating in confusion of what was going on. He saw the masked person being carried out and thought they were going to send away John instead of Axton, which was true, but they believed it was Axton in the same mask.

Thunder roared across the sky as the torch-bearing crowd gathered in a circle. "Wait!" screamed Howard. "You have to stop this!" Howard took a swing at one of the elders as he pushed through the crowd, but he was quickly overpowered and shoved down on his knees to watch. Howard's face was filled with pain at the sight of his star pupil being banished.

"Pavana tanaya sankata harana," started the leader of the group with his hands held up in the air. "Mangala murati roop," the man continued. There was another clash of thunder and the doorway started opening up beneath John.

"Stop," John whispered to himself, not telling them but commanding time. Everything froze except for John and Howard. John stepped out of his restraints and walked over to Howard. Then he spoke, "Do not cry for what has been done or what we are to become. There is still one yet you must teach." Handing a slip of paper to Howard, John continued speaking. "You will need this. It will be his first lesson. The man who frees you from your prison."

As tears fell from Howard's eyes, he looked up at the Masked Man who was beyond any of this and spoke, "I'm sorry. I am so sorry. I shouldn't have neglected everyone else for you. Forgive me." Howard's version of what had happened was egoic. He blamed himself.

John brought his face much closer to Howard and spoke. "He will come to you. You must teach him. He is to become your best student. Then we will both be forgiven." Upon finishing his sentence, John focused his connection and sent Howard to the circle in his place before resuming time. With a look of shock on everybody's face, it was too late to stop. John stared toward the spot where he knew he would be viewing the memory. There was a scream from Howard that seemed to be pulled out of the very fabric of the universe as his body disappeared completely and the Masked Man was left standing there.

Everybody in the crowd took a step back in fright, fearing what was coming next. "Howard!" screamed the man who Howard had said was his brother during the memory. "No! Howard! Come back!"

"Stop!" John shouted, this time commanding the panicked crowd. Some of them tried to confront him, but John pushed their attacks to the side with little effort. John took off his mask to show them who he was, for the first time. There was a gasp from the people who could see through the darkness and confusion.

"It's not Axton," said one of them.

"No, he is the Adamant One," another replied. The crowd quickly turned to the other man with the mask, and realized that he was the one they should be afraid of. The mask Axton was wearing burst into flames and Axton started hovering above the ground bursting with energy and power. They had doomed themselves without even knowing it. The Temple and surrounding buildings started exploding and catching fire one by one. People were bursting into ash all around as their energy was sucked away into Axton. John held his hand up to Axton, and the surrounding energy stopped. Gravity took hold and Axton fell three feet back to the ground, the skin on his face started burning from the fire and energy.

"You can't stop me," Axton said to him. John lifted his other hand, and a few inches above it there was a glowing orb that started making a whining noise. Axton stood up, looked at his foot, and let out a cry of pain as it started turning to bronze. What seemed like an eternity for Axton, was only a minute or so in reality. Axton was completely frozen in bronze. The crowd stopped and stared at the sight they had just witnessed. They were relieved that the threat was gone, but their fear was turned toward John.

"My son!" Jeff yelled as he ran outside. He had been lying in bed flying through the universe through the commotion but had been brought back by the burning buildings and explosions. Jeff ran to the statue of Axton and fell to it's feet crying. "Axton!" Jeff yelled at the statue, but before he could finish, the statue and John disappeared. John had taken them to the Chateau. He stood outside of the silent building with his frozen comrade and stared off into the distance, letting everything sink in.

After a few days at the Chateau, John sought out anyone who was ready to connect with the other side. He offered them the opportunity to live there, where they could leave the fake world behind, and focus on oneness. It is in this way that he came across Jimmy, who had recently left The Library and become young again. John appeared to his younger self in the bathroom mirror and explained that he would be able to do this one day. It was incredible living out the experience from another point of view. John would never get over how cool it was to talk to himself. Even from this more powerful side of it. The awe inspiring action of

John's energy lead Jimmy to give him the moniker of Master. John explained what needed to be done in order for Jimmy to be saved from The Library. John put on the mask and together they went to the coffee shop where they played out the scene John had described to Jimmy. They froze Mary Jane in time and left, after sending young John to the beach. John spent the majority of his time teaching his followers and meditating, up until the day he would take a seat at the throne in the main hall and wait for Mary Jane to come in while young John freed Axton.

Chapter 25

John Kills Himself Again

The events played out as described earlier in this book, but now John was on the other side of things. It made more sense now why he said the things he did. It had been John who was building the whole story in the first place, but there was no way he could have known that when he was young. John wondered if there was some way he could explain everything to his younger self or Mary Jane to prevent his death which was approaching by the minute. There was just no way to stop it and still let everything progress up to this point. This is how it happened, and it has to happen for everything else to happen, John thought to himself, wishing there was another way. He knew exactly how young John would attack him and kill him. It would be simple to overpower him or avoid the attacks, but it would change everything. What would happen then? What would happen to his own existence if he changed this crucial moment in his life? It was a gamble to the existence that he had, here and now. Even if it was his own death that he had to face, at least he had lived up to this point. He could tell Mary Jane about it and maybe she could talk some sense into him, but that would change everything. Maybe she could just stop him right before the final attack, but it didn't happen that way. I was there and I lived it as young John. So that is how it has already happened. It's just not possible to do anything else. I have to face this so that everything falls into place, as it was meant to be. It has to. There is no other way.

There was no time left now. John had to face his own death. He started counting down in his head. Ten. He called Mary Jane into the main hall to send her back. Nine.

"Before I send you back, I have to tell you that I know you and Jimmy gave the book to John and started all of this," said John.

"We had to," Mary Jane started to say defending her action.

"It's okay, it had to be done. I wanted to thank you for being here with me all of this time. I know it wasn't the easiest thing to do, but it had to be done. I hope you understand it all now."

"It is the only way it could have been," said Mary Jane. Eight.

"One more thing before you go, who do you think wrote the book?" Mary Jane looked at him puzzled. "I wrote it, well, created it at least." Mary Jane only had a second to look amazed before there was a flash and she was no longer in the Main Hall talking to future John. Jimmy was in the room with him. He handed the mask to John. As he put on the mask, John was at Seven.

Young John appeared in the main hall to confront him and Jimmy stood in front of the masked John to protect him. Six.

"It's okay, Jimmy, You may stand down, it is all right," said John through the mask. "There is only one way this can end, John."

"That's right," said young John, "I am here to kill you. You are going to pay for what you did." Five. Young John started throwing energy at the Master with the intent to kill him. Masked John blocked his attacks and threw his own at young John. Four. He knew that he couldn't really hit young John with the attacks, and threw them into the exact places he remembered dodging them. It had all been a big setup, only this time he was in on the joke. Three. Young John got close enough to him that they were even throwing fists at each other. Two. Masked John was mimicking the moves he remembered were performed, like an actor in a play perfectly choreographed. His younger self was exerting himself, in an intense battle of uncontrolled emotion while masked John moved with ease through what he already knew. One. With a final scream, young John shoved his hand against masked John's chest and threw everything he could at him. He stood there and took it. Masked John collapsed to his knees then fell to the ground. It hurt as much as he imagined it would. The anger and hatred of his own hand forcing energy into his chest.

Mary Jane appeared at the Chateau just in time to witness the final violent blow. "No!" her screams echoed as she ran over to the dying Master. There was very little time left. Through the mask, John sprayed out blood as he laughed.

"This is how it had to be," he said. "This is how it always had to be."

"John, how could you do this? Why didn't you talk to me first? Oh John," Mary Jane said with tears streaming down her face, "you shouldn't have." She was crying and holding the Masked Man's head in her lap. "I'm so sorry."

Masked John coughed again and said to her, "take off my mask. It is time to show him." Mary Jane lifted the mask off of his face, and young John was filled with a sense of dread. The face under the mask was his own face staring back at him.

"He is you, John. *He* is who you are going to become," said Mary Jane. John was the Masked Man. It had always been him. It had to be him.

"No," young John said horrified. "No…"

Masked John used up all the energy he could to smile one last smile at John and speak to him, "I forgive you, John. It had to be this way. After all… you are going to be me. That is your punishment." Everything went dark for masked John as he took his final breath.

Mary Jane broke down completely. Young John went over to her but she pushed him away.

"No! Don't touch me. You are a monster!" Jimmy stood by shaking his head and people started filing into the main hall to see what had happened. They formed a circle around young John once again and started moving toward him.

"I didn't know…" young John said, "I didn't know." As the followers got closer to him young John shut his eyes and vanished from the main hall. The Chateau was quiet except for the sounds of Mary Jane crying as the followers stood watching in silence.

"I'm so sorry," Jimmy said to her. "I don't know why he wanted it this way."

"I should have told him sooner," Mary Jane said sniffing. "Oh John, how could you do this? We're supposed to be the good guys."

A thunderous sound of electricity pierced through the sobbing and a doorway of light appeared only a few feet away from John's body. Through the doorway stepped a tall man with a black goatee. The followers took a step back from the blinding light and powerful energy that was emanating from the doorway. Shielding her eyes, Mary Jane squinted to look at the figure who was walking toward her and John.

"It's you," Jimmy exclaimed. The man smiled a large grin, towering over them. Light was pouring from his body like someone having a continuous waterfall above them.

"Uncle Howard!?!" Mary Jane exclaimed.

"We can save him," Howard said, walking over to John's body, "give me your hand." Mary Jane had so many questions for her uncle: where had he been, how did he get there, what happened! This wasn't the time to ask them. John was lying there dead. "This isn't how I wanted us to be reintroduced, but I am his teacher, and it is up to me to protect him," Howard said to Mary Jane. "Put your hands on both sides of his head." Still holding John in her lap, Mary Jane put her hands on his head. Howard knelt down to John's body and put both of his hands on John's chest. The light in Howard grew so bright the followers had to look away. There was light coming from his entire being. Mary Jane felt the warmth that was coming from him. Then Mary Jane stopped being Mary Jane. She connected completely, leaving her self behind. She could see the energy coming through her hands into John. As soon as it had started, the energy from Mary Jane stopped. Howard removed his hands and the light faded back into his being.

John was lying still while everyone looked on intently. Then his eyes shot open and his head flew back with a horrible scream, "Aghhhhhhhhh!" John gasped for breath, remembering what it was like to be on this side. John's whole body was shaking. He looked around at everyone trying to take in what had just happened. He could feel the disruption in his energy as it pulsed through his body.

"Howard?" he said, noticing that he wasn't on the beach. "What happened?"

"It's okay, he helped bring you back to me. Howard is my uncle. He told me he is the one who has been teaching you. Oh, John, I was afraid I had lost you," Mary Jane said, not sure where to start.

"How did you get here?" John asked Howard.

"I was freed when you died, John. Just as it was written. When I felt it, I knew I had to come here to save you. I told you that you would make great mistakes, John. I didn't tell you that I would be there to help you correct them." Howard waved his hand to the doorway and another man walked through. "I want you to meet your father John. I took him away and saved him after you left your childhood bedroom. It's okay, John. You are the hero of this story. Mary Jane couldn't have picked a more perfect partner."

Mary Jane held on to John tightly, not even letting him get up off of the floor before hugging him tightly.

John's father spoke to him, "It's okay, John. Howard told me everything. I know what happened wasn't your fault. I am sure we have a lot more to catch up on, but as soon as you are feeling better we have to save your mother. She has suffered long enough, not knowing the truth. I want you to know I am proud of the man you have become. I couldn't have taught you about this state of existence as well as Howard has, and I thank him for that. Not everyone could handle the trials that you have gone through, including sacrificing yourself for the greater good. You have grown up to be more than I ever could have imagined."

"And Jimmy," said Howard, answering his thoughts. "Yes, I am the same man who took you to The Library. It was all at John's request." A long awaited question finally explained itself. Jimmy nodded speechless.

"Howard," said John calling him closer, "…I am sorry."

The world went dark again for John after Howard replied, "think nothing of it, I would only blame you if I thought it was your choice in the first place."

Chapter 26
Saving Lives

Mary Jane gave John as much space as she could for him to rest, but halfway through the next day she could not help but go to see him in bed.

"Thank you," John said. "Howard told me how you helped save me."

"John, you are my world now. I would do anything for you," she said.

"I'm sorry for leaving like that… and for not telling you I was going to confront the Masked Man. I mean me."

"You should be sorry, especially for dying on me. I won't put up with losing you anymore." They both smiled and kissed each other. "Now get some rest," she told him as she started to walk away.

"Can't you stay with me?" John asked her sincerely.

"Oh, if I have to," Mary Jane replied sarcastically as she climbed into bed with him.

When John had fully recovered they decided to go back and get his mother from the institution. John went alone with his father because they didn't want to bring too many people at once. It was a cold and empty place. They allowed John and his father to visit with her. John told them his father was his uncle because they knew the family history and would have started asking questions if they had been honest. They decided his father would go in first so he could prepare her to meet John. They didn't want a repeat of the last time John had tried to visit. When John's father walked in, his mother stared at him in amazement.

"You are here to take me away," she said. "I am ready to die. I can't take this place another second."

"No, it really is me," his father told her. "I am here to take you home and I brought John too, but there is something you have to know."

"Where have you been, I saw you die..." his mother said, desperately wanting to understand. She was on a lot of medication and had spent the last few decades of her life being convinced she was crazy, but had always hoped that one day someone would believe her.

"It is a long story," said John's father. "It would be better if I show it to you, then you can meet John."

"My son?" she said to him. "I have been waiting my whole life to know my son."

"Close your eyes," John's father said to her. He put his hands on her head and they were both still and silent for a moment. In a second, his mother was back to normal. She saw the whole story in her head and understood all of it. The drugs were taken from her body along with the experiences she had in the institution.

"Gregory!" said John's mother with tears falling from her eyes, "I saw it all. Where is my son? I want to see him." John had already been watching them from afar. He went to his mother who promptly hugged him and never wanted to let go.

"I saw you show her everything," John said to his Dad. "You are connected with the other side aren't you?"

"I am John," his Dad said, "it runs in the family. We have always been outsiders. It is no surprise that you are too. Now, let's get out of here. Can you take us away?" There was no admitting to what they saw on the security tapes at the institution that day. It was attributed to a glitch that three people were there one second, and gone the next. The status of John's mother was marked: *unknown* and she was never seen there again.

John could not have been happier. His family had finally been reunited, he met the girl of his dreams, and he was living in a mansion with no need to ever work again. Everything seemed perfect for the first time in John's life. He was a somebody, and he was saving people from the restricted world they created for themselves. When everything settled down, Jimmy came to him one day and asked for a favor. "John, I want to go back to The Library," Jimmy said. "It is so hard to have lost access to all of that knowledge. I know it can be challenging to never leave, but I think it is worth it."

"I know what you mean," John said. "I didn't create The Library just to keep Axton there, it was meant as a repository for all the world's knowledge. Having to keep it closed as a jail cell does not do justice to it's existence. I will take care of it for you."

John went to his father and told him there was something he would need his help with. They went to The Library together to confront Axton. With his renewed encouragement from Howard and his family, John was confident that he would be able to save Axton. As they entered The Library they found Axton sitting at a desk reading. "So, have come back to gloat," said Axton, "or give me a second chance to kill you?"

"We are going to help you Axton. This is my father. He will help you and you will be free to go," said John.

"What is to stop me from leaving right now?" Axton asked him.

"I think you know that I'm not the same person who left you here, Axton. I have lived through all of the events that made me stronger and have already been the person who froze you in bronze," John said, not threateningly, but as if it were common knowledge that he was much stronger now.

"I figured as much," said Axton. "I doubt the other you would have had the guts to come back here. Go ahead and get it over with."

John's father put his hands on both sides of Axton's head and closed his eyes. This might be a weird sight to most people, but for those who can see beyond, there was light moving through both of them. John's father took away all memory Axton had of the book so he would never find out he could take power from others. Axton would be harmless from this point on. As the creator of The Library, John was free to take off the restriction that one person had to be there at all times, though Jimmy would often be found there. Axton and the ghost of his father joined John's following, and could be found together meditating by the bronze statues. Axton didn't remember the time he had spent as one of them, but he would often be in the same spot as he had been as a statue, as if some trace of memory remained. John focused his connection and joined all three of the other dimensions into one. The Library was now part of the Chateau, which was overlooking the beach. He also restored and connected the Temple to the Chateau, for the more dedicated followers and teachers to continue their practice. In the Chateau, John found Jimmy waiting for him in the Main Hall.

"How did it go?" asked Jimmy.

"The Library is open to the public once again," John said. "In fact it is now part of the Chateau. I made a copy of the key for you, though it never needs to be locked. Go take a look now, there is someone waiting for you there."

Jimmy's face was filled by a big smile as he took the key from John. He went into The Library and back to the office he had been using while he was trapped there, wondering who could be waiting for him. As he walked closer he noticed the figure of a woman standing in the doorway. He started to cry almost instantly as he said her name and ran toward her, "Victoria!" She now looked the same age that he did. The couple was reunited in their youth. John had saved Victoria and brought her back to The Library as her younger self so that they could be together.

If Jimmy hadn't been at the point of worshipping John, there was no doubt now. As John would later say to him, "I knew you weren't going to use the cure on her and that we had to meet at The Library with just you there, but you have been loyal and faithful to me and have been nothing but the best of additions to this world. I expect I will be able to find you both together in The Library any time I need you."

Chapter 27
Loose Ends

John and Mary Jane couldn't have been happier. They were finally in a place where they could spend their lives together and help others awaken, but there were still people left to invite to this paradise. They decided first to invite Mariela, nature lover, the girl who could fly. They both appeared before Mariela at Arches through their new found traveling system of connecting with the other side.

"You have come a long way, but at the same time haven't moved at all," said Mariela. "I would hate to disappoint you in whatever it is you need. Now go ahead and ask." She cut straight to the point.

"As you may know, we have been through a lot in the time since we last saw you. We would be honored if you would join us at our newfound paradise that I have created," John said to her.

"Ah yes, I have heard a lot about this paradise of yours," Mariela replied. "It overlooks the beach doesn't it? And I hear it has the world's largest Library. It sounds very nice, but you must know I already have my own paradise created right here, by me. In fact, I have not moved for two hundred years besides getting closer and farther from the ground, if you consider that moving, I mean. Remember that it is all an illusion when you want most to hold onto things. You must sense that it is not the truth."

"I think we both knew that you wouldn't come with us, but nevertheless there will always be room for you, if you decide you need a change of scenery," John said to her.

"Maybe I will come there for vacation," Mariela replied to them. "It's always good to see you John, in person I mean. We are all together beyond this world."

John and Mary Jane closed their eyes and traveled together to give out the next invitation. This time it would be Mary Jane doing the talking, as it was her parents they were going to invite. She imagined they would be thrilled to find out that Howard was alive and well. It's not every day that you connect with long-lost members of your family. Mary Jane's father, Bill, was definitely older than the last time John saw him (at the Temple trying to banish Axton), but it was certainly the same man, Howard's brother. When Mary Jane told them about Howard, the look of shock on the faces of her parents was unparalleled, but it didn't have as much happiness in it as Mary Jane had expected. "How is that possible?" her father asked.

"It's a really long story, and most of it is hard to believe, but come to the Chateau with us, and I'll tell you all about it," said Mary Jane.

"Why are you lying to us?" her father asked. "Do you know how hard on me it was when he disappeared?"

"I'm not lying," said Mary Jane.

"It's true," John interrupted getting between them. Her father was angry, like someone was playing a cruel joke on him after all of these years.

"You know your father is touchy about the subject, why would you tease him like that?" her mother asked.

"But Mom, it's true," Mary Jane said. "I'm not lying."

"Maybe we should have brought him here with us," John said to her, trying to calm things down. "We can go get him."

"No!" her father shouted. "I won't believe this. This is insane. What has this guy you've been hanging out with (meaning John) gotten you into? He is turning you against us. Can't you think for yourself? I thought I raised you better than that." Mary Jane had tears in her eyes at this point. She just wanted them all to be happy and everything was going wrong. John was comforting Mary Jane, holding her while she cried. Her father was standing up and pointing aggressively at this point.

"I think it's time we leave," John said, standing up for them with a tone of strength and command, "and when we come back, we'll bring Howard with us." Upon hearing John say he would bring Howard, Bill's face changed drastically. It went from anger to fear.

"No, there is no need for that... it can't be him, I'm sure it's not my brother," Bill said suddenly a lot nicer to John. What was this about, John thought to himself, why is he afraid to see Howard? The change in tone made it clear that Bill already knew that Howard was alive, and John had been there when Bill sent Howard to the beach by mistake. Was he worried that Howard would be mad at him for it?

"I think I *will* bring him here," John said with a serious voice, "that or you can come visit him at my Chateau."

"You have a Chateau?" Mary Jane's mother asked him, surprised. It was rare in their town that you would meet or even hear about someone owning their own Chateau. She would really have been impressed if she knew it overlooked the beach. Something tells me Bill wouldn't have been as pleased to hear that part.

"All right," Bill said, "we'll go with you and prove that it isn't him. How do we get there?"

"Just close your eyes," Mary Jane said, trying to be helpful. "John, take us there." Bill reluctantly closed his eyes, not expecting anything to happen.

"Well, this is the stupidest thing I've done in a while. We are supposed to just magically appear there, huh?" Bill said, but when he opened his eyes again, they were all standing in the main hall of the Chateau. "Well I'll be..." said Bill, "you must have slipped something in my drink when I wasn't looking. This is unbelievable."

For a change of pace, Howard was the one sitting on the throne awaiting their arrival. Jimmy and Victoria were nearby, expecting the return of John and Mary Jane. Jimmy was still very protective of John, even though he knew that John was more than capable of standing up for himself, and that was an understatement. John could rule the world. He could manipulate the universe at will. Any great ruler would be hard pressed to stand up to John in a fight.

"Ah, welcome. It's been so long," Howard said. Then he stood up and ran over to Bill to give him a big hug. "Brother! I never thought I would see you again in this lifetime," Howard said to Bill, who was more being hugged than exchanging a hug. Bill was still surprised to have traveled to the Chateau, and seeing his brother again... he didn't know how to react. Howard finally let go of him and looked at Bill waiting for him to speak. Slowly a smile appeared on Bill's face and he raised his arms to hug Howard back.

"Howie, how are ya, where have you been all this time?" asked Bill.

"You must remember at the Temple, I was sent off to another world. It was actually a beautiful world, a beach where time stood still. In fact, the beach is now part of the grounds of this very Chateau. It's an incredible story really. I was finally set free when John died, and with Mary Jane's help, we were able to save him," Howard started explaining. It was at this point that John noticed the age difference between Bill and Howard. Bill had been living out his life on a normal timeline, while Howard had been stuck in a timeless space and was noticeably younger, even though he had surely lived as long.

"Wow, I didn't know what happened to you after you disappeared," Bill said, "but it was because of John that you were stuck there, isn't it?"

"Well... in a way, yes, but I don't blame John for it, everything happened the way it was meant to. There was no other way for everything to fit into place," Howard replied.

"You are lucky you weren't there to see what happened... it was chaos... death and destruction. I almost envy you for that," Bill said to him with a fierce look. Then he noticed that no one was following along with his train of thought and quickly changed the subject. "But you are back now! I can't believe it! I never thought I would see my brother again. You rascal."

"John has been kind enough to allow me to extend the invitation to both of you to stay at the Chateau with us. Oh, and you'll have to excuse me, you haven't introduced me to your lovely wife," Howard said.

"Ah, where are my manners, Howard, this is my wife Jane, our daughter was named after her. Jane, this is my brother Howard," Bill said, introducing them to each other.

"It is a shame I missed the wedding," Howard said. "It is such an important event in life to get married... and even more so, I missed the birth of my own niece! Time flies by sometimes. I hope all of you know that I do want to be a part of your lives again, especially Mary Jane, who I would like to take as my next student. The things she has done would amaze you. Bill, she clearly gets it from you. I could even teach Jane some of this if she is interested." Bill was a bit taken aback upon hearing that Mary Jane was so involved. He had done his best as a parent to protect her from the life he had fled.

"Oh, I wouldn't know where to start, I'll leave that to you young people, but we would be happy to stay with you for a while, wouldn't we Bill?" stated Jane happily. "Bill has always been talking about going on vacation. Now it won't cost us a thing, and we will get to be with his brother, our daughter, and her boyfriend."

Bill feigned a smile, "Yes, that would be just great. I can't wait to spend more time with them, especially you, John. We have a lot to talk about if you're going to be with my daughter."

Chapter 28
Revelations

Things carried on at the Chateau quite smoothly for a few days. Everyone seemed to be getting along. Howard started teaching Mary Jane the advanced materialization techniques, and Mary Jane's parents were enjoying walking around the grounds, as well as the tour Jimmy gave them of The Library. After a few days, Bill finally managed to get a minute alone with John to talk to him.

"It's time I tell you the truth John, I never thought I would run into you again. This time I made sure it was on my terms. I have been orchestrating all of this, from the moment you met Mary Jane. You think my daughter would fall in love so fast with a stranger just because he can do a few magic tricks? You're deluding yourself. The only reason she even talked to you in the first place is because I told her to," Bill said to him. "She has been working for me this whole time."

"No, you're lying..." John said trailing off at the end. His head was spinning.

"It is our job to stop people like you. People who think they can do whatever they want. No one person should have as much power as you do. Look at all the people you have hurt, even yourself! I can't let you hurt anyone else," Bill continued.

"What do you mean..." John said, "how is that possible?"

"It's all your fault, John. You are responsible for all of it. The death and destruction. The pain and the misery. You couldn't be happy with your life so you involve everyone else in your torment."

"What? What can I do?" John asked him sincerely, believing every word of his lies.

"There is something you can do. You need to disappear. To be gone from here. Somewhere you can never hurt anyone again. Here," Bill said, opening his hand toward John to hand him the gold orb of light. "If you really love her, you will do this."

John slowly held out his arm toward the light. He took it in his hands and stood up with his head slightly bowed and his eyes closed. John didn't make a sound even though it must have been painful for the light to turn him into bronze, his senses were dulled from losing the only person he cared about. Bill grinned. "That was easier than I thought it would be," he said to himself right before Howard burst into the room.

"Bill, what have you done? I felt the disturbance," said Howard. Then he noticed the statue of John. "John? How could you do this to him? Why did he let you? We have to change him back!"

"*We* don't have to do anything, Howard. This was the plan all along. Do you think we were fooled for a second by Axton wearing the same mask back at the Temple? We wanted to send John away all along, that's why we couldn't let you be a part of it. Especially after you went crazy over that book," Bill said.

"This isn't right Bill, you are my brother! He isn't hurting anyone. You were always jealous of anyone who was stronger than you, is that what this is about? You must know how much stronger I am, are you going to kill me too?" Howard shouted at him.

"Howard. I hoped you would understand this. We are blood. Family. This murderer shouldn't be set loose on the world. Look at all the destruction he has caused," Bill replied calmly, but clearly disappointed. "You are my brother, Howard. I love you, it killed me to lose you, but you must know how much calmer things have been since then. I have a family now and I don't want them involved in any of this. As soon as John is out of the way I will make them forget he ever existed and we can go back to being a happy family."

"You are a coward," Howard said to him angrily. "You have always been weak!"

"Don't follow me Howard, or you won't be lucky enough to land on the beach this time," Bill said to him with a dark look in his eyes. Bill and the statue of John disappeared.

Howard jumped through space after them. Bill and the statue of John appeared on the roof of a castle that was high up in the mountains. John was still present in the statue. The view was beautiful. It was one consolation he had to being frozen in bronze. That and plenty of time to think. Bill looked up for a second in thought. "He didn't listen," Bill said, as if John could still be an active conversational partner. Bill walked calculatingly a few feet away and stood waiting. Howard appeared on the roof facing John with Bill less than a foot behind him.

"John, we have to fix this," Howard said, but he was interrupted by a sharp pain as Bill quite literally stabbed him in the back. With his arm around Howard's neck, Bill pushed the knife he had created into Howard. Howard gasped and Bill slowly let Howard fall to the ground in his lap. Bill comforted Howard and gave him a small kiss on his forehead.

"I am sorry, brother," Bill said. Howard couldn't speak, but was looking up at his brother with hurt in his eyes. Howard never thought Bill would be capable of anything like this. "I told you this would happen. You were supposed to be gone," Bill said. "Why didn't you stay away?" Howard closed his eyes and let out one last exhausted breath. Bill pushed Howard's body off of him and stood back up. He walked over to the statue of John and spoke to him, "You see the trouble you have caused? This is all because of you. You create nothing but death. Now if you'll excuse me I have to turn my daughter against you." Bill disappeared from the roof. A single tear fell from the statue of John. The intensity of emotion he felt watching Howard die was enough to manifest a real tear on the bronze statue.

Chapter 29

Fear

"John. John, where are you?" Mary Jane asked aloud as she walked through the halls of the Chateau. It was quite a large building, but Mary Jane didn't usually need to make an effort to find John, even if he was somewhere well hidden. They always found each other when they wanted to just by thinking about it, but today was different. None of the followers seemed to know where he was either. Mary Jane spent the better part of an hour looking for John before she talked with Jimmy to see if he had any knowledge of his whereabouts. She didn't phrase it like that to him, of course, because she was not a 1950's detective or police officer. It was something more like, "Hey, Jimmy, have you seen John? I have been looking all over for him."

Jimmy replied as everyone else had, "No, I haven't seen him. Have you checked in his room?" Jimmy wasn't paying as much attention to the situation as he should have been until Mary Jane made it more clear.

"I have been looking for him *everywhere*. I have never had to look for him before, and suddenly it's like he's gone."

"Oh. I see what you mean. That is strange. Anytime I try to find him, John usually comes to me. Give me a second to concentrate and see if I can find him." Jimmy closed his eyes for a minute and put his two first fingers on either side of his forehead. "Hmmmmm," he said as if he were thinking deeply, "he's not here."

"He's not here?" Mary Jane asked, as if it would be strange for that to happen, which it would if you were Mary

Jane, because John never went anywhere without her anymore, and they seemed happily situated at the Chateau. On top of that he had not mentioned anything to her.

"He's not here. Not at the Chateau at least… or The Library… or the beach… or the Temple. He's not here on this plane with us," he told her.

"Where could he be? Why would he leave without telling anyone?"

"I suppose there are many reasons someone would do such a thing, but I've seen the way he is around you, and I don't understand it. Maybe we should wait longer and see if he arrives."

"Jimmy, you aren't getting it. You know how time works here. John could be gone for a hundred years and he would be back in only a moment of our time. The only reason he would be gone is if something happened to him."

"Let's not jump to conclusions…" Jimmy trailed off, knowing she was completely right. "Let me try again." Jimmy concentrated once more and after a little while of humming he opened his eyes again and said, "This is very peculiar, I can't seem to find him anywhere. Which could mean a few things: either he doesn't want to be found, someone is blocking him, or… something bad may have happened to him."

"What!" exclaimed Mary Jane rather loudly.

"Don't worry, John can take care of himself, wherever he has gone. I'm sure he'll be back in no time and all of this worrying will seem foolish," Jimmy replied. But there was a look on his face that betrayed what he was saying. Jimmy was worried too.

"What are we going to do?"

"I don't know that there is very much we can do. I will look through The Library to see if I can find any answers. In the meantime do some of the meditation techniques and see if you can connect with the other side."

Mary Jane left The Library to go to her favorite meditation spot at the Chateau. There was a ledge overlooking a beautiful garden with flowers always in bloom. Mary Jane had cushions placed around the area for others to enjoy the space as well. She sat down and closed her eyes when someone sat down next to her and spoke.

"Are you all right, dear, I saw you run out here like someone on a mission." It was her mother, Jane. Mary Jane saw who it was and started opening up to her mother, who was always sympathetic when Mary Jane needed someone there for her.

"Oh Mom, John is missing! I looked all over and can't find him anywhere. Jimmy said he isn't here anymore."

"That is very strange," said Jane. "He seems like a really nice guy, and I know how you two feel about each other. I'm sure everything will be okay. It's just like that time you were little. Do you remember when you got lost at the store and thought you would have to live the rest of your life without me? It probably seemed like forever but it was less than ten minutes that we were apart."

"Mom, I'm a lot older than that now. Things like that don't happen anymore. I feel like his energy is being blocked. Even Jimmy has tried his best and can't find John."

"Don't worry dear. What is the use in worrying? What can I do to help you find him?" Jane asked.

"I don't think there is anything you can do, but thank you for listening. I need to meditate and see if I can find a connection with him and the other side."

"I'll do it with you. Maybe if we both do it then we'll reach something faster."

"Okay, Mom," Mary Jane said knowing that her mother was being nice, "just close your eyes and let go."

"Okay, sweetie, I'll try not to bother you while I do it." They both sat there meditating trying to see if they could find a connection with John. The echo of Mary Jane calling out for John was all that Mary Jane heard in her head. John….

John…

John…

John…

Where are you John? Can you hear me? Bill stormed out into the garden feeling the cry from his daughter.

"What are you two doing out here?" Bill asked them as if he didn't know. "Jane, don't tell me you're getting mixed up in this stuff too."

"We're looking for John, he has disappeared and we can't find him," Mary Jane responded.

"You're wasting your time," said Bill, "he doesn't want to be found. There is something I have to talk to you about, come inside with me. Jane, I think it will be easier if I talk to her alone."

"What aren't you telling me?" Mary Jane asked as she got up from her meditation position.

"Calm down honey, come with me and I'll explain everything. I talked to John before he left," Bill said trying to encourage her. Mary Jane agreed and followed him inside to her bedroom. When they got there Mary Jane was taken aback that things were out of place. Someone had been looking through her things and tried to place them back properly.

"Now, I know what you're thinking and don't get mad at me," Bill said. "I went through your things, but only because John asked me to. He said you have a book for me and that I should get it from you."

"That doesn't make any sense, why would he want me to give *you* the book," Mary Jane said to him.

"John said it was dangerous and could hurt people, and that I could take it somewhere safer. I hate to tell you this, but that is why he left. He was worried he was going to hurt more people. You saw how he even hurt himself. John is somewhere that you will be safe from him. He said he loves you, but it needs to be this way," Bill said to her.

Mary Jane listened to her father and concentrated the book into her hands. She handed it to him and said, "I have to talk to him. He is confused. I know he would never hurt anyone on purpose."

"Dear, he knows how dangerous all of this is, that is why he wanted me to take the book from you. The things it does are not safe, and should be forgotten," Bill replied. Then it clicked. Bill thought that the knowledge was contained in the book. Mary Jane remembered Jimmy telling her that the information from the book stays with you, even if you don't have the physical copy. If Jimmy knew this, then John knew this, and something was terribly wrong.

Bill skimmed through the book, which was nothing but blank pages to him.

"Hmm," said Bill, "tricky little thing isn't it? I'll make sure no one gets hold of it again."

"Will you take me to John now? You have the book. I need to talk to him about this."

"I'm afraid his decision is made. I promised him I would never go looking for him or send anyone after him. I didn't tell you this, but he did something else much worse than you can imagine. I watched as he killed your Uncle Howard.

It was the hardest thing I have gone through in my life. And I had to watch as I lost him again. John has too much power and he doesn't know how to control it. Your uncle knew that and look what happened when he tried to help."

Mary Jane was shocked. Not only had her uncle just been reintroduced into her life, but he was accidentally killed by John? It didn't make any sense. None of this made sense. She had to find John.

"Now, promise me you won't look for him anymore. It is what he wants, and you deserve better," Bill said to her, "we can all go home tomorrow and forget about all of this."

Mary Jane agreed so that he would leave the room and she could find a way to John. Bill hugged her and smiled as she said, "Okay, Daddy." He walked out of the room and Mary Jane sat on her bed thinking of what she could do next. The book was still with her, even though Bill had taken the material version of it. As long as she had access to it's knowledge, than she would find a way to make this work. She just couldn't let her father know what she was doing.

Chapter 30
By The Mountain Pass

Mary Jane didn't know how much time she would have before her parents, specifically her father, decided they would be leaving the Chateau, and taking her with them. It seemed certain that she would not be allowed back there. Mary Jane didn't know what Bill was capable of, but she feared the worst at this point: that she would be locked away in a small room and never allowed to interact with human beings again. That may have been a bit drastic, but with a vengeful coward like Bill, who knows what is possible? If Mary Jane knew the truth about him, and what he had done, then she would already be in fear for her own safety. She was quite convinced that there had to be a way to find John. Who wants to give up on their soul mate, after all? Mary Jane didn't know if people really had or could meet their soul mates, but this was the closest she had come to a relationship with someone that seemed like they were meant to be in her life. Ah, what an impossible notion it seemed to be to find John. Even with all of the knowledge the book had taught her, Mary Jane didn't know where to begin in finding John. If Jimmy could connect and found nothing after having lived for hundreds of years, how was she supposed to do it?

Mary Jane looked through all of her things trying to find something that would be useful. Toothbrush? No. Dirty socks? No. It didn't take long for her to look because she had not moved very much of her stuff into the Chateau at this point. She had left most of her material possessions in her past life both physically and mentally. Mary Jane was losing hope by the minute until she saw it. A small box under her bed. She picked it up and looked at it hesitantly. Please let there be some left, she thought to herself, even though she dreaded going through with this. Mary Jane knew it wasn't the safest, or even most fun way to get where she needed to be, but it was her only hope at this point. She opened up the box to find that there were two chocolates left. They were the same ones she offered to John when they first met. She knew they would take her somewhere... but she didn't know where. It would be hard to keep track of herself while she was under the influence of the chocolate. It was still a mystery to her what was inside of them that made everything the way it did. Jimmy had prepared this batch and given them to her for John. She knew this was her only shot at finding John, so taking a deep breath and holding her nose, she ate both pieces. She needed a strong dose. They tasted completely like dark chocolate but the mind plays tricks when you know what you are doing, even if it seems pleasant. Things were about to get interesting for Mary Jane.

She sat down in an easy chair across the room and started to feel herself melting into it. That was the feeling she was having, not the reality. To an outside viewer there was just a girl slouched in an easy chair. To her everything was being pulled downward. Gravity had grown to a massive proportion and every part of her felt heavy. She was losing track of time. She was losing track of herself. There was a voice that Mary Jane heard, she would speak aloud, but it wasn't someone identifying as Mary Jane who was speaking. Her thoughts would go from one topic to another, wandering and finding answers where the question had not been spoken, but they were all the right answers. To an outside viewer, this would appear frightening, but not to Mary Jane who was now the voice.

"Everything makes sense now," she said, "it all makes sense. Why don't people see it? Why don't they know it? Everythingness. It's everywhere. But it's not real. Things seem like they are real. Everyone wants their things to matter to you and you have to act like it back. They don't understand. They don't get it. Everything. They missed the point. I don't want to be here anymore, but I don't want to die. I am not here. There are a few of us here. Is there anyone else here?"

"Good question," was spoken aloud through Mary Jane's mouth, though it wasn't her thinking anymore. Secrets of the universe and other side were spilling out of her mouth past her mind which was no longer in the picture. "I can save him," she heard her mouth say. Her head was silent. "Save who? Save me. There is no me. I'm not that. I don't identify with it. I shouldn't be it. Why does everyone know what they want to instead of what is? They have their version of everyone else and they can never really be with them, they can just be with themselves in that person's presence. That's why they are never happy. I am just projecting my own fears. I am too hard on myself. It is hard. This is easy." Mary Jane was losing track of reality as we know it, and not in the way that she had been for the past few weeks, but in a new way where she was no longer in control of it. Everything suddenly felt lighter, like she would float out of the chair, even though the journey was getting more and more intense. The chocolate was doing it's job and taking her beyond the endless beyond.

In a moment of clarity she spoke, "John. Where are you?" Mary Jane found herself standing on the roof of a building looking out over a vast beautiful stretch of mountains. The feeling was one of overwhelming beauty. She was crying, but it wasn't her crying. Tears were going down her face from her eyes but there was nothing but love.

"Mary Jane," said a voice behind her, "what are you doing here?"

Mary Jane turned around to see who was talking to her and saw the bronze statue of John. Next to the statue was a figure of John who was talking to her.

"John!" she said, running over to him and holding him, "what happened?"

"Well... I'm stuck in a statue," said John.

"But you're right here hugging me," Mary Jane said. The part of her mind that was still functioning did not understand, while the rest of her being was glowing with the perfect nature of everything.

"Yes and no," John said. "My physical being is trapped in that statute. This is just a projection of my consciousness. It was getting stifling to just see in one direction so I popped out to meditate."

"But I'm touching you."

"Yes. That's because this is a projection of your consciousness too. We can interact as if we are both really here because neither of us are in our bodies right now," John explained to her. "Why did you come here?"

"John, why did you leave me? I love you so much. I don't want to live without you in my life. You didn't even say goodbye," Mary Jane said to him, still crying, now partially out of sadness.

"You love me? Really love me? He lied to me. I agreed to be frozen here to protect people and because he told me you weren't really in love with me. None of it is true, is it? How could I not see that sooner? It was so hard for me to believe that someone like you would love me... and I know I've hurt people..." John said.

"I love you, John! I have loved you from the moment you ordered my coffee for me. We both know the connection we have. We were sent here knowing that we would find each other. How do you think it was so easy for me to get here to you? It's love, John. I don't care what you have done by accident, including killing Howard, I know it was never something you did on purpose. I know you could never hurt me, John."

"I was such a fool to believe a word of his lies. Wait, you think that I am the one who killed Howard? How did you even know he is dead? I didn't kill Howard, it was your father who killed him. He is the one who told me that you were working for him and didn't really love me. He told me it would be best if I left everyone so they would be safe from me."

"My father?" Mary Jane asked. "He really did this? He killed his own brother? Why would he do that?"

"He is afraid of anyone with more power than him. He will stop at nothing to make sure that he never has to compete with me."

"That's terrible. I can't believe he would do something like this. I am so sorry John, I should have never brought him here."

"I don't blame you, it is my fault for listening to him. I should have talked to you before I agreed to let him do this to me. You have to save me. Get me out of this bronze." Mary Jane went over to the statue and put her hands up to it. Light emanated from her hands but nothing happened.

"It can't be done with consciousness alone. You have to come here and do it in person."

"I will do anything," said Mary Jane. "Where are you and how do I get to you?"

"I've been here before, in what feels like a dream or past lifetime. I can tell you how to get there if you just concentrate." It was too late. Everything started to fade and Mary Jane found herself falling back into her body in her bedroom screaming. She was back at the Chateau and the chocolate had worn off. It was over six hours later than she had started. Everything felt tight again, like she was crammed back into a small package. Her body was shaking from the energy. She could feel the intensity of this new energy with every beat of her heart. Jimmy was in the room just in time to catch her as she leapt out of the chair.

"It's okay, you're safe, you're here at the Chateau," Jimmy said, holding on to her. "You shouldn't have eaten the chocolate alone. Especially this dosage that was meant for someone of John's stature."

"I had to find him, and I did... I saw him. I talked to him. But... but, I don't know how to get where he is. It is on top of a building overlooking mountains."

"Wow, that is incredibly lucky. Someone is looking out for you. There was a chance you wouldn't wake up after having so much of that chocolate... well... at least not as you. It has a tendency to make people lose themselves, which is good if they need to connect with the other side, but coming back is not always easy. I wouldn't even have given them to John if I didn't already know the story of him taking them."

"So how are we going to find him? Should we just start looking where there are mountains?"

"No, that would take a dreadful long time, assuming he even is in what you used to call the real world. I was actually just coming to find you because I know of a way, but there is a catch. I found a connection that can take us to John, but you have to have someone who has been there in order to open the gateway. How are we going to find someone who has been there?"

"More good news then. I found out that my father is the one who took John away. There is a good chance that he went with John. We can use him to open the gateway whether he likes it or not."

Jimmy's face got dark as he understood the betrayal of someone who had been invited to their home as a guest. Someone so close to the family. He might have lost it completely if Mary Jane told him about Howard's murder.

"He will be lucky if that's all we do with him," Jimmy said. "We better do this in the morning so I can calm down and control myself."

"Agreed," said Mary Jane. "It would be best if we have a plan before confronting him. We don't know what he is capable of. I still can't believe he would do something like this. After all the good times we had together when I was young. I never thought he *could* do something like this."

"There is so much that we don't know," said Jimmy. "That is the first lesson I learned when I was asked to work at The Library so many years ago."

Chapter 31
Bill & The Book

Bill sat in a chair in one of the guest rooms looking at the book contemplatively. He wanted it's power. He reached forward and picked up the book, which had been lying on the coffee table in front of him, and flipped through it again. The pages were still blank. "Where's the on/off switch?" Bill said rhetorically to himself. What was he supposed to do to make it work? He put it down again and kept staring at it. He focused on the book and concentrated, furrowing his brow and squinting at it. After a few seconds he relaxed his face again. "Open sesame," he said aloud. He lifted the cover of the book with one finger to see if somehow that was going to make it work. It didn't. The pages were not revealing themselves to him. Bill still didn't understand how the book worked. He thought he knew, it held great power, but just like any other book in writing for someone to read. That was not the case.

"Come on dammit," he said to the book, "show me what you've got." He was getting frustrated at the book. Then he tried sweet talking it, "Come on book. You are such a beautiful book, you are. I bet you would like it if someone real nice picked you up and flipped gently through your pages. How about it?" The book sat there and didn't move. That's what most people would expect from a book but this was frustrating to Bill. He took a deep breath and let out a long, "Hmmmmmmmmmmmm," which made anything not bolted to the floor start shaking. It was a long, drawn out sound that would have made anyone stop in their tracks. The book didn't care. It sat there like any other book. Bill looked at the pages once again finding that they were still blank.

"All right," he said, "enough. Have it your way. If you won't show me, then I won't let you show anyone." Bill walked over to the fireplace, every few paces looking back to give the book a dirty look. He took a few logs from next to the fireplace and stacked them on top of each other inside of it. It was a wood burning fireplace but it did have a gas starter. Bill turned the key for the gas to start and used his trusty lighter to get it going. He walked back to the chair and sat in front of the book while the fire built up. "That's it," said Bill, "this is your last chance." He waited a few more seconds then flipped through the book. There was nothing in it. Bill reached his arm up in anger as if he was going to throw it across the room, but remembered he had something else planned for it. He walked over to the fireplace with the book in his hand. "It's a shame really, to lose such sacred knowledge," he said. He slowly put the book toward the fire.

The book, still in Bill's hand, started glowing. It wasn't on fire. It was angry. Bill tried to throw the book into the fire but it wouldn't let go of his hand no matter how hard he shook it. He even put it far enough to burn his own hand, crying out in pain before pulling it back out of the fireplace. He flailed his arm with the book still attached. "Get off me," Bill yelled at the book. He tried to use his other hand to pry away his fingers one by one but he couldn't get it out of his hand. Then he felt the book pulling itself into his arm. It became distorted as it slowly integrated itself with him. This process doesn't have to be painful, but for Bill, the book made sure it was. Bill was yelling and clenching his wrist as if he could stop it like you would water in a hose. He couldn't. Then it all stopped. He stood there no longer in pain with nothing but the fire crackling to be heard. He held up his hands and looked at them. Nothing. The book was gone. "I guess this is what I wanted," Bill said, "show me something." Nothing happened.

Bill was about to walk out of the room when he heard a voice from someone sitting in the chair.

"You are a coward," said the man, "you have always been weak." The color left Bill's face because he recognized the voice and the words. He slowly walked around to the chair to see who was sitting there. As pale with fear as he was, Bill was the picture of perfect health compared with Howard who was sitting in the chair with an angry look on his face.

"You're... you're not really here," said Bill, trying more to convince himself than Howard.

"You think you can control everyone don't you?" asked Howard. "I guess they never told you John is the one who created the book. It was made from pieces of the other side. Infinite energy and knowledge all in one neat little package. It's alive you know. It is alive and it was going to let you off easy but you had to push it, you had to dominate it! Now you've made it angry, and you'll get what you really deserve."

Bill was sweating and had completely lost all of his nerve at this point. He ran from the room just as Jimmy and Mary Jane were coming to confront him. Jimmy grabbed his arms and held him in place while he was screaming about someone being in the room. "No, get him away from me. Let me go," yelled Bill. Mary Jane went into the room but there was no one there. She turned off the gas to the fire and looked around the room to see what Bill had been doing in there, but she could find nothing. Bill was still freaking out as Howard's ghost was now walking right toward him and there was no way Bill could escape because Jimmy was holding on to him firmly.

"What's wrong with him?" Mary Jane asked.

"I don't know," said Jimmy struggling to keep ahold of him. The ghost of Howard walked right in front of Bill and put his finger on Bill's forehead. Bill went limp and his eyes shut.

"I think he passed out," said Jimmy, "Help me get him into this room." Jimmy and Mary Jane dragged Bill's unconscious body into the room and put him on the chair.

"Get me something to tie him up with," said Jimmy. "I'll make sure he doesn't go anywhere." Mary Jane left the room with a slight jog that implied importance but would not be overexerting. Jimmy paced back and forth in the room thinking. The part about Bill being upset was going to be expected, but Jimmy thought it would come after they told him they knew everything. Jimmy was turning around to start walking the other way when Bill jumped up from the chair and pushed him across the room. Jimmy fell against a table and on to the floor. Bill ran out of the room before Jimmy could get up. Mary Jane heard the noise and ran back to the room, this time making a complete effort in a more drastic situation.

"He went that way," Jimmy said, pointing in the direction Bill had fled. Mary Jane ran after him and found him at the end of a hallway. He was humming and holding his hands out. By the time Mary Jane could run to the end of the hallway, Bill had disappeared.

"No," said Mary Jane angrily. "He can't get away from us!"

Jimmy had started chasing after them down the hallway. He was at the other end of the hallway coming toward Mary Jane.

"Don't worry, he did just what we needed him to do. If he opened the doorway to John, then we'll be able to reopen it in the same spot and don't need him anymore."

"Assuming that is where he went. I just hope he didn't go to the world of spikes or something."

"Is that a real place?" Jimmy asked her.

"I don't want to find out if it is... What do we need to open the doorway?"

"It's just a matter of time," said Jimmy, "I'll start working on it now."

Chapter 32
A Losing Battle

Bill appeared on the roof of the castle relatively far away from the statue of John. He was just happy to have gotten away from the Chateau where there was a dead man following him. Unlike having most dead men following you, this one had the added impact of being one Bill himself had killed. That makes it much more unimaginably terrifying, as Bill found out, when such a rare event occurred to him.

"This is all your doing," Bill said to the statue of John. "I don't know if you like being a statue, and I hope you don't, but let's see how much you like being a statue without a head!" Bill stood for a moment then was suddenly holding a large axe. Apparently he thought that would be the best way to behead a statue. Clearly he wasn't in his right mind, and even if he was, what would you choose for beheading a statue? Probably a blow torch or electric saw. As Bill stepped closer to the statue his vision started to get blurry. He fell down, partially from the weight of the ridiculous axe, but mostly because of whatever it was taking over his head. He stood back up, determined to do what he came here for but now there were statues of John all over the roof. Everywhere he looked, he was surrounded by the statues of John. Bill knew there was only one real statue, but they all looked the same. How would he be able to differentiate them?

"I can't trust my eyes," said Bill. He closed his eyes and stood for a moment trying to feel out which way to go, but he didn't want to take another step forward because he knew he was on the roof of the building and if you put two and two together, Bill would not survive the fall.

"You are a coward," said a voice in his head, "you have always been weak." Bill could smell his brother's cologne. He could feel the breath on the side of his face. Bill didn't dare open his eyes now. Tears of fear were welling in his eyelids. He dropped the axe then fell to his knees crying defeated.

"Stop," he said. "Stop. Leave me alone. I don't deserve this. I just wanted to protect my daughter."

"What's wrong with him?" Jimmy said. He and Mary Jane were on the roof of the castle watching Bill break down crying.

"Help me fix it," said Bill with his eyes closed. In his mind, Howard was towering over him. He was talking to whatever it was in his head more than any real person there. "I can fix it. I can make it all better if you'll let me, please help me. I promise to behave."

Mary Jane would have been taken aback by this scene if she had been paying any attention to Bill. When she arrived on the roof she ran straight for the statue of John. She was hugging it tightly, which the bronze didn't mind at all. Mary Jane concentrated on John and bringing him back. Slowly the statue started to come back to life. The eyes opened into real eyes and the mouth opened to a real mouth which took in a deep breath that John had been wanting.

Jimmy walked over to Bill cautiously, trying to help him and calm him down.

"It's okay, there is no one here. What are you afraid of?" Jimmy asked.

"No, get away from me," said Bill. "All of you get away from me! It was me," he continued crying. "I killed him. I killed Howard. I killed my brother." Bill fell over and was lying on his back sobbing.

Jimmy and John looked at each other wondering what they were supposed to do with what was left of this man.

"Help him, John," said Mary Jane. Being the bigger man he imagined of himself, John took the initiative to go over to Bill to try to see what was wrong. It struck him immediately in the core of his being.

"He has the book, and the book isn't very happy with him," John said. He climbed on top of Bill and put out his hands at Bill's chest. There was a glowing light and then the clear outline of the book turned into the real thing in John's hands.

Bill gasped, "Thank you! Thank you so much. I'm sorry. I'm sorry for everything I did." Then Bill opened his eyes and looked at John as if seeing him for the first time.

"Who are you? How did we get here?" Bill asked John, his emotion had gone from fear and sorrow to confusion.

Mary Jane looked confused until Jimmy spoke to her on a side note, "The book took what it needed from his mind. He will be a better person from now on."

"I am your future son-in-law," said John. "I am going to marry your daughter."

"She couldn't have picked a better man," said Bill, "but what are you doing on top of me? Will you please let me up, young man?" John got up off of Bill and helped him to his feet. John handed the book to Jimmy with a knowing glance. Jimmy accepted it into his protection once more. John closed his eyes and in a moment they were back at the Chateau. Bill seemed to know where he was but the details were fuzzy. Something about John working for a big tech company and making millions at a young age. He must have slept through the plane ride.

John and Mary Jane finally had time to talk alone in her room at the Chateau.

"Thank you for what you did, John," said Mary Jane. "He is my father... but I don't know if he deserved saving after what he did."

"It's not up to us to decide," John said. "I did what was right and what I was supposed to do."

"Are you really going to marry me?" asked Mary Jane. "That seems like something you should ask me before you go on assuming."

John laughed, "I hope so. Mary Jane will you do me the honor of being my partner for the rest of our lives? When I say that, remember we may very well live forever."

"Of course I will, John," said Mary Jane giving him a big hug. "After almost losing you again, I can't see myself living without you."

"This is the greatest day of my life," said John, "No, I take that back. Every day with you is the greatest day. And to think, it all happened because of that one little word, Apertambuxtion."

Prologue

We see a young and naive version of John walking into an electronics store.

"Can I help you young man?" one of the clerks asks him.

"Yes," said John, "I think so. I need to buy a computer."

"Well is it for business, school, or personal use?" the clerk asked him.

"A bit of all three," John said. "I don't know very much about computers, and I have a somewhat limited budget."

"I'm sure we can find you exactly what you need," the clerk said, "come with me to the computer department." The clerk spent time with John explaining which models were which, but John was confused with all of it. Then the clerk spoke to him in a more mysterious manner, "You know what? None of these are right for you. I have something in back that will be perfect. It is brand new, top of the line, an experimental model. I can sell it to you for a really good price because we ordered so many of them." The clerk went into the back for a few minutes and came back with a lightweight portable computer that John fell in love with right away. "It's very easy to use," the clerk said pushing the power button, "you just turn it on like this and enter the password. This one has been preassigned, but you can change it if you like. I'll write it down for you so it's easier to remember." The clerk scribbled something on a piece of paper and stuck it to the computer.

"It's just some made up word that nobody will be able to guess. You know how security is these days. Apertambuxtion.

That's it. Just type that in with a capital 'A' and you're on your way to all of your computing needs."

John thanked the clerk for all of his help as he was checking out. He had gotten a great deal on exactly what he needed. If only salesmen were so helpful everywhere he went.

After John left the store, the clerk's appearance changed quite drastically. Instead of the store uniform, he was now wearing a cloak. He had become a tall man with a dark goatee. Howard stood there, then grinned for a moment before disappearing.